The Consignment Shop

Pat Dolce

TM&P

Tandem Media & Publishing

The Consignment Shop

Pat Dolce

FIRST PRINTING

ISBN: 979-8-9889241-0-4
eBook ISBN: 979-8-9889241-1-1

Library of Congress Control Number: 2023914827

TM&P
Tandem Media & Publishing

This is a work of fiction. Names, characters, places, and incidents either are the product of the author's imagination, or are used fictitiously. Any resemblance to actual persons, living or dead, businesses, companies, events, or locales is entirely coincidental.

For author inquiries, please contact TandemBooksUSA@gmail.com.

To my precious son, Lowell. You are, without a doubt, the most wonderful human being I have ever known. You couldn't possibly make me prouder than you do every single day. Your accomplishments never cease to amaze me. You are the light of my life and I love you beyond words! I also can't thank you enough for bringing Carlton into our lives; that precious little guy truly is my best little friend, next to you of course!

1

Nadine Horton was not herself and hadn't been for a while. Not since the accident.

It had started out as such a pleasant summer day. Nadine had gone, with Madam, her little Maltese, to her sister Sandy's house, a twenty-minute drive from her home in their quiet little Connecticut town. Nadine and Sandy weren't just sisters; they were twin sisters, and thus connected in that strange, mystical way that only twins can understand. They had a wonderful day gardening and then having lunch on Sandy's back deck. Ah, how they loved these days together, making all their favorite foods from childhood and sharing all the latest "juice," as they called it. Sandy always had the latest gossip about everything. Years before, Nadine had taken to calling her "Hedda," a reference to Hedda Hopper, the famed gossip columnist of the 1940s.

"And now for the surprise dessert I made last night," Sandy said after lunch. "Mom's famous rice pudding! Try as she might, it was never as good as the deli's!"

"Not even close!" Nadine laughed.

The pair chatted away, and finally Nadine gathered up Madam and said her goodbyes, telling Sandy to drive carefully later that evening.

"I still don't understand why you don't wait until the morning to go see your daughter," she remarked. "Get a fresh start. It's a two-hour drive, you know."

"I told you, Nay," Sandy said, "we want to have a full day tomorrow to paint. It's a big apartment, so I need to get there tonight."

"Well, stay alert. There's a lot of crazy drivers out there, Hedda."

"I know," Sandy smiled. "I will. I'll grab a cup of coffee for the road. Speaking of which, thanks again for the coasters for the cup holders. Every morning when I spill my coffee on them, I'll think of your compulsive neatness!"

"Oh, you're welcome. Just a little token gift for your new car. Let me know how they work out."

"I will!"

"And text me when you get there."

"For sure."

Then they'd warmly embraced, and Nadine and Madam drove home.

Alan made dinner that night. He was a wiz in the kitchen, and Nadine loved his spaghetti Bolognese.

He'd been making it for them for thirty-six years, as long as they'd been married. Afterward, they went into the den to watch TV, and it was right about then that Nadine felt something strange washing over her. She felt warm and then hot. She found it hard to breathe. She was clammy. Alan noticed right away.

"Honey are you okay?" he said rising from his chair and moving over to the sofa where she was sitting. "You look a little pale."

"I'm... fine," she said. "I'm sure I'm fine. Just a little woozy. Probably from that second glass of wine I didn't really need."

"Let me get you some water."

The spell, whatever it was, passed quickly, and moments later, Nadine was quite all right. Nevertheless, it unnerved Alan. He'd never seen his wife like that.

"Nadine, I want you to call Dr. Buffa in the morning," he said. "You haven't had a physical in years and you keep putting it off. We've got a lot of traveling ahead of us and I need you to be up to it!"

Indeed, Alan had recently sold off his chimney cleaning business of thirty-two years, and the plan was to finally take the time to see something of the world.

"Alan, I'm fine," Nadine said.

"I still want you to get your physical."

Nadine sighed. "Okay, okay, I will."

It was an hour after that when the phone rang with the terrible news.

After the shock of the tragedy had diminished to where she could think somewhat straight again, Nadine would realize that the official time of death was the exact time that she'd had the strange spell. She knew it wasn't the wine. That was only something she had said to keep Alan from worrying.

Sandy had died en route to the hospital. Her car had veered off the road and then hit a tree, apparently at a very high rate of speed. There were no skid marks. There were no witnesses, either. A driver had spotted the wreckage just moments after the accident happened and called 911.

Six months later, Nadine was still reeling. She wasn't sleeping. She wasn't eating well. Alan had been patient with her, but he knew she needed help. He gently suggested that perhaps she could talk to someone. A therapist, or maybe Reverend Berry at the church. Truthfully, he missed his wife. He missed the fun-loving woman she was before the accident, and he wondered if he'd ever see that woman again.

Nadine declined the suggestion. How was talking to someone going to make things better? Sandy was gone, and no amount of talking about it would ever change that simple and incontrovertible fact. She said as much to Randy, too, their thirty-year-old son who lived in Cape May, New Jersey. Randy had come for the funeral of his aunt but had had to get back to his job at the bank right afterward. He felt bad about not being able to spend more time with his mother, but he did make it a point to call her just about every day, and, like his father, he felt that opening up to a trained therapist could help Nadine immensely.

Neither Alan nor Randy pushed the matter, both figuring Nadine would be ready in her own time. But Alan did enlist the help of some of Nadine's friends, all of whom were as concerned about her as Alan was. Colette from the book club called to encourage her to come back, and so did Jackie from her mahjong group. "We miss you," they both said.

Nadine did go back to book club one night, and she did play mahjong another night. Still, it was a struggle for her, and on both occasions, she came home feeling exhausted.

Her friend Claire from down the street had called every day since the funeral. Alan sure appreciated that. Good old Claire. One night, she called and told Nadine she was going to take her out to lunch the next day and would not take no for an answer. Nadine didn't especially want to go out, but some small part of her—a very small part—did want to feel something approaching normal again. So she invited Claire over, telling her she'd make her patented barbecue chicken salad sandwiches. It was the first genuinely productive thing she'd undertaken since the accident, and she had to admit it felt good to prepare a meal and entertain a friend.

For her part, Claire brought over Scrabble and a bottle of wine. She brought something else, too—an old pendulum board that she'd come across in a consignment shop, a wooden board with the letters of the alphabet engraved on its surface in an antique script, along with the numbers 0 through 9, and two small boxes, one that said "Yes" and one that said "No." Claire had a pendulum, too, and she explained to Nadine how divination pendulums typically work. You rest your elbow on a table and let the pendulum hang down on its chain from your hand. You ask it questions. The pendulum, reputedly a conduit between this world and the spirit world, answers in different ways. It might start swinging back and forth, or maybe side to side. Maybe it'll start swinging in a clockwise, or counterclockwise, direction. One movement might mean "yes." Another movement might mean "no." But a board creates the conditions for more specific answers with less guesswork needed on the part of the person holding the pendulum. "You can ask it anything," Claire declared, "and get *real* answers!"

Just like Claire, Nadine thought. She believed in all that stuff. Claire wore scarves and turquois beads and hoop earrings. Nadine loved Claire dearly, but she always looked like some leftover Bohemian from the '60s. She talked endlessly about "auras" and "energy" and the power of crystals. Of *course* she would bring a pendulum and a board.

Claire suggested, ever so kindly, that, perhaps, if she wanted to try it, Nadine could use the board to communicate with her departed sister. "Listen, Nadine," she said, "if nothing else, it might be good therapy."

"I don't think so, Claire," said Nadine. "I appreciate the thought, but it's really not my kind of thing." Then she chuckled and said, "I mean, what are we, kids?"

"Oh, I knew you were going to say something like that!" Claire laughed. "Well, I'll tell you what, I'll leave the board here in case you change your mind. And if you don't, you can take it back to the consignment shop where I got it and exchange it for something you'd like. It's a great little shop with some interesting things. I bought myself a beautiful little throw rug that I saw next to the board, which goes perfectly in my upstairs hallway. Anyway, if you see anything you like, it'll be my gift to you."

"Thank you, Claire. That's very kind of you. Is it the shop on Garner Street?"

"Yes, that's the one. Have you been?"

Nadine nodded. "I stopped in there a couple of months ago. I bought Sandy some pretty coasters for the cup holders in her new car..." Her voice trailed off and she looked off into the distance.

Claire struggled for something to say. "Yes...yes, that's the place," she said. Then, trying to sound cheerful, she added, "Feel free to exchange the board for anything you like!"

Nadine turned back to Claire and forced a smile and then Claire suggested Scrabble and soon the pair were lost in the game. They played Scrabble, ate sandwiches, drank some wine, and had a lovely afternoon. Aside from that one moment thinking of Sandy's accident, it was the best Nadine had felt since. Nevertheless, not long after Claire left, Nadine slipped back into her grief, going to bed early and sleeping in late.

When she finally came downstairs the next day, she was dressed and ready to drag herself to the consignment shop. She retrieved the pendulum board from the dining room table where she and Claire had been sitting the day before and poked her head into the den where Alan was watching the news.

"I'm going out," she said.

This seemed like a good sign. "Oh?" said Alan. "Where to?"

"Just to the consignment shop where Claire got this."

"What is it?"

"A pendulum board."

"A what?"

"Nothing. Just something silly Claire brought over. She said I could exchange it for something else."

"Do you want me to come along?"

"No, that's okay. I won't be gone long."

At the shop, the owner told Nadine, "Sure, you can exchange it for anything you'd like. We haven't paid the consignor for it yet, so that makes things easy. They have some other interesting things here, too. Follow me." The woman walked Nadine over to booth "15," and she put the pendulum board back where it had been sitting when Claire had purchased it a few days before. There was a rather large and eclectic mix of items, old and new, in booth 15, and, in fact, Nadine remembered finding the coasters she'd bought for Sandy in the very same booth.

"See?" said the woman. "These people must have been cleaning out their whole house. A little something for everyone. Well, feel free to look all around the store. Just let me know if there's anything I can help you with." Then the owner of the shop retreated to the counter.

Nadine did look around the store but soon found herself back at booth 15, unable to take her eyes off a pair of heavy bookends sculpted into the shape of gargoyles. She'd never seen anything quite like them. They were at once grotesque and beautiful. She ambled about the store again, and then returned to the bookends, knowing she had to have them. It was a strange purchase—she and Alan didn't have many books—but somehow, the bookends seemed to be calling out to her, and surely she'd find a place for them.

Alan said very little about the purchase when Nadine came home. The bookends certainly weren't anything he would have bought, but Nadine appeared pleased with them, so that was good enough for him.

In fact, Nadine was so pleased with the bookends that she returned to the consignment shop the next day to see if she could find anything else of interest. This time an antique table lamp struck her fancy, also from booth 15. It was all copper with a decorative dome, and, like the gargoyle bookends, she couldn't take her eyes off it. She brought it home once again to Alan's lukewarm reception.

"Do you like it, Al?" Nadine asked him.

"Oh, sure," he said. "I like it. But if you like it, dear, that's all that really matters." And he meant it. Nadine's mood seemed to be picking up, and as far as Alan was concerned, she could buy the whole damn consignment shop if it gave her something to smile about.

In fact, Nadine surprised Alan the next day with a very positive announcement. "Al, I've been thinking; I *would* like to talk to someone."

"You would?"

"Yes. I would."

"That's great, Nay. I think it will help. I really do. Well, listen, I hope you don't mind, but I've made some inquiries. You know my friend Mark? Well, his wife went to see a psychologist named Dr. Sharma when her mother died. She specializes in grief counseling, and Mark says she was a ton of help. I have her number. What do you think?"

"That sounds fine, Al. Can you call and set up an appointment for me?"

"Sure I will."

Nadine started seeing Dr. Sharma twice a week. Alan was curious how the sessions were going, but Nadine didn't seem to want to share any details and Alan didn't press her.

The funny thing was Nadine had continued to visit the consignment shop from time to time and Alan noticed that she seemed happier coming home from there than from Dr. Sharma's office. Within a couple of weeks, she'd bought an old oil painting—a seascape with two wooden sailboats. She'd also bought a large stained-glass picture of a starfish, a steel fireplace tool set, a portable ice maker, a pair of flameless candles, and an antique birdcage. This last one was a bit of a mystery to Alan, seeing as though they had no bird.

"But look at the intricate wirework," Nadine had said. "I'll put a plant it in or something."

The purchases didn't even make a lot of sense to Nadine. What was it about the objects from the consignment shop, each one of them, strangely, procured from booth 15? Nadine somehow found them comforting. On some level, only vaguely apparent to Nadine, they felt safe. They were of the past and they spoke to her of a more secure time, a happier time, a time when the world made sense and you could depend on things. A time when people you loved didn't die suddenly for no reason in random car crashes.

One day she came home from the shop with a present for Madam, a matching dog bowl and leash, both with red, white, and blue stripes. Whether Madam noticed the difference when she ate her food out of the new bowl that night, who can say, but Nadine was satisfied with the new acquisition. She washed it out good the next day, however, as Madam had become ill later that night, vomiting up her dinner. Had the bowl been unclean? Nadine had rinsed it out, but now she scrubbed it and even disinfected it. Madam vomited the next day, too.

"Oh, poor baby," Nadine said to Madam. "We'll just have to take you to see Dr. Winston, won't we?" and she made an appointment to see their veterinarian for the following day.

Nadine would miss that appointment.

After she called Dr. Winston's office, she called Claire, realizing that she hadn't heard from her since...well, when was it, anyway? Two days ago? No, it was three days ago, Nadine realized. Claire had been calling every day. How strange that Nadine hadn't heard from her in the past three days.

She rang Claire's cell phone but got no answer. She tried later that day with the same result. She texted. Nothing came back.

Alarmed, Nadine walked down the street to Claire's house. Claire's car was in the driveway, but when she rang the bell, there was no answer. That's when Nadine called the police for a wellness check. An officer arrived fifteen minutes later, knocked loudly on the door, walked all around the house seeing nothing suspicious, and then forced open the front door.

And there was Claire, lying at the foot of the steps.

Nadine collapsed.

The officer checked for life, but Claire's body was cold, her neck broken from the apparent fall. Paramedics arrived to tend mostly to Nadine who was conscious but in shock. They took her to the hospital where the doctor on duty gave her a sedative. Alan came and got her and brought her home later that evening.

A full investigation was done at Claire's house, headed up by Detective Simon Barker of the local police department, but the death was ruled an accident. One of those freak things. Claire had apparently tripped on a throw rug at the top of the stairs, lost her balance, and tumbled down the steps.

Nadine barely said a word for three days after the discovery of Claire's body, rarely coming out of the bedroom. Alan thought that if she'd made any progress since Sandy's death, it had all been erased. If anything, she was worse. He was at a loss. Nadine refused to go see Dr. Sharma, the one person Alan felt might be able to help. He called Dr. Sharma himself asking what he could do for his wife. "Just be there for her," Dr. Sharma said. "But please stay in touch with me. She's in an extremely fragile state right now. If necessary, we can make arrangements for in-patient care."

On the fourth day, there seemed to be a break in Nadine's mood. She came downstairs that evening for dinner. She didn't eat much, but when Alan asked how she was, she said, "I feel okay." Then she actually smiled a little. "I think everything's going to be okay now," she added. "We're both going to be okay."

They went to bed that night with Alan finally feeling some hope for his wife of thirty-six years.

Three days later, on a wellness check prompted by Randy, who hadn't been able to reach either his mother or father, Alan would be found still in bed where he had had those hopeful thoughts, his head split open, presumably by the fireplace poker found at the feet of Nadine, who was found hanging by a red, white, and blue dog leash in the bedroom closet.

2

"A murder-suicide? Really?"

Nicole Anders, twenty-three years old, slim-figured, and with long brown hair that matched her eyes, was trying not to sound too excited. She was a professional, after all. A year before, she had been only a student, a journalism major at the University of Connecticut. But since then, in the twelve months she'd worked as the *New Liberty Gazette*'s crime beat reporter, returning to her hometown after graduation, she'd seen nothing more newsworthy cross her desk than a convenience store robbery. A murder-suicide? In New Liberty? This was *big*.

She rested her Starbucks cup on her tiny desk. It was still early, not quite 8:30 a.m., normally a quiet time in a quiet town.

"That's what the police radio said," Walt Massey replied, standing in the doorway of his office. It was Walt, Editor-in-Chief, who'd hired Nicole. The *Gazette* had been in the Massey family for three generations. Now it was barely hanging by a thread. Like a lot of small-town papers, the internet had been a curse. Print subscriptions were down to almost nothing. Most of the revenue came by way of advertising on the *Gazette*'s website and it was just enough to keep the lights on. Fifty-seven-year-old Walt, heavyset with black-rimmed glasses, had had to let pretty much everyone go. Nicole worked as the crime reporter, food critic, and arts and entertainment editor. Besides Nicole, whose salary as a cub reporter was semi-affordable, Walt kept old Clint Holloway around too. Clint, pushing eighty, had been a hire of Walt's father, and Walt couldn't bring himself to consider laying him off. Besides, Clint worked for cheap. He just wanted to work and to somehow remain relevant. He covered local sports, politics, and business news. Walt covered everything else.

"How long ago?" Nicole asked.

"Just now," Walt replied. "I heard it come over the radio right before you walked in the door. A 10-63. I had to look it up. I don't remember hearing one before."

"Wow."

"Don't bother to even take your jacket off. Go check it out pronto and see if you can get a statement from the police. Barker's probably there and I'm sure he'll talk to you. Tell him I said hey." Walt scribbled the address on a piece of notepaper and handed it to Nicole. "Now get going."

Nicole rolled her eyes, put the paper down, and snapped a picture of it with her iPhone. "Walt," she said, "it's 2023. Nobody carries around little scraps of paper anymore."

Now it was Walt's turn to roll his eyes.

"Okay, I'm off!" Nicole said, racing toward the door with her coffee and phone.

"Call me as soon as you know anything," Walt called after her.

"I'll text you, Walt. I don't know if I'll have time to talk."

"Well, send me some form of communication!" Walt yelled, but Nicole was out the door.

Out in the small parking lot adjacent to the office, Nicole jumped into her 2015 Jeep Wrangler and headed toward the address. She chuckled, thinking of Walt's technophobia. Then again, it wasn't such a laughing matter. If Walt would only let her do some of the things she wanted to do to bring the paper into the twenty-first century, maybe the *Gazette* could recapture some of its lost glory. She knew that the key was to engage readers in better ways online. She'd talked to Walt repeatedly about developing an app for phones and tablets, using tracking software to target readers with content relevant to them, or at least updating the *Gazette*'s website. It looked like it had been developed in the nineties. She'd volunteered to spearhead every improvement, knowing the efforts would look good on her resume, but Walt kept putting her off. "One of these days," he kept saying, but Nicole suspected that "one of these days" would arrive too late for the paper's survival.

Fifteen minutes after leaving the Gazette's offices, Nicole pulled up to a colonial-style house on a quiet, tree-lined street. There was no need to double-check the address. Two police cars and a forensics van parked out front were all the confirmation she needed.

A statement from the police, Walt had said. Nicole wanted to do better than that. She genuinely liked Walt and, technologically deficient though it was, she liked working for the *Gazette*. She'd grown up with the paper, after all. As a little girl, she read the comics religiously, along with the syndicated Dear Abby column. But the *Gazette* was a mere stepping stone for her now. What she needed was a collection of serious news articles with her byline that she could send off to the newspapers she really wanted to work for. Top of the list: The *New York Times*. Of course, that was probably down the road. There would have to be a couple of stops in between. The *Hartford Courant*, maybe? Or something like the *Newark Star-Ledger*. That would get her closer to New York City. But either way, nobody was going to take her seriously with a string of credits that included features on restaurant openings and fluff pieces on art and seafood festivals, that was for sure. Nicole wanted to be an investigative reporter. A serious journalist. The next Diane Sawyer or Christiane Amanpour.

She got out of her Jeep and ambled up the walk to the partially open front door of the house. Crime scene tape was strung across the porch, but she managed to peek inside just long enough to be noticed by a uniformed officer who strode toward the door and barked, "Crime scene!" before shutting the door in Nicole's face.

"But I'm with the *Gazette*! I work for Walt Massey," Nicole yelled to the closed door. "Can I get a statement?"

Hearing nothing from inside, Nicole walked around to the back of the house, trying to see into the first-floor windows, but the curtains were all drawn. The rear door was locked. She stood for a second, glancing around, looking for some hint of what happened inside, but the back of the house could have been the back of any house in Connecticut. Nobody could have guessed a murder-suicide took place inside.

Nicole walked back around to the front.

"Miss?" someone called out. She turned to see a neighbor woman walking her terrier. "Why are the police cars here? Do you know what happened?"

"I'm told it was a murder-suicide," Nicole replied. "But I can't confirm that."

"Oh my God!" said the neighbor, a forty-something woman with long, light brown hair. "What? The Hortons?! Nadine and Alan? A murder-suicide?!"

Nicole grabbed her reMarkable tablet and stylus. "I'm sorry, did you say the Hortons?"

"Oh, I just don't believe it! Never in a million years. They were the nicest couple in the world."

"Did you know the Hortons well?"

"Well, sure, they were here when my husband and I moved in ten years ago. Oh, God. A murder-suicide?!"

"Well, again, I can't confirm it," Nicole said. "All I have is very preliminary information. You see, I work for the *New Liberty Gazette*."

"Oh, I see. Hmm...I didn't know the *Gazette* was still around."

Nicole winced. "We're alive and well, I assure you. Do you mind if I get your name? For the article?"

"Of course. It's Janice Browne. Browne with an 'e' on the end."

"Uh-huh. And how old were—what did you say?—Nadine and Alan?"

"About my age. Fifties."

"Did you know of any history of domestic abuse?"

"Domestic abuse?"

"Yes, I mean, were the cops ever called here? Did the couple fight? Did Nadine ever talk about Alan hitting her or anything like that?"

"The Hortons? Oh my God, no. They were lovely people."

"Health issues? Depression? Anything of that sort?"

"No. Well, of course, Nadine's twin sister recently died."

"Oh?"

"Yes. Car accident of some sort. Nadine was devastated about it, but that's only natural."

"Of course."

"My God, I just can't believe this is happening! And right after Claire's death."

"Was Claire the sister?"

"No, no, Claire was another neighbor. See that little Cape Cod at the end of the block? The one with the blue shutters?"

"Yes."

"Claire Collins lived there. A week ago, they found her body at the bottom of the stairs. Just an awful thing."

"Oh yes, I remember that," said Nicole, recalling the bulletin that had come in from the police department. "She'd slipped and fallen, or something like that. No foul play. Just a tragic accident. I didn't realize it was the same street. How odd."

"Yes, isn't it? You know, now that I think about it, it was Nadine who had called the police for a wellness check on her."

At that moment, the front door of the Horton house opened and New Liberty police detective Simon Barker stepped out of the house. Barker was in his late forties, tall and fit with graying hair and a square jaw.

"Well, thanks," Nicole said to Janice. "You've been very helpful." Then she raced over to the detective.

"Good morning, Nicole," Barker said. "I figured you'd be here. I guess you need a statement, huh?"

"Good morning, Detective. Yes, I do, thank you."

"How's Walt?"

"He's doing just fine and sends his regards. But what can you tell me about what went on in there?"

Barker took a breath. "Well, not much to tell. Murder-suicide."

A murder-suicide and there was not much to tell? Nicole had a hard time believing that. "The Hortons, right?"

Barker nodded. "Alan and Nadine."

"How exactly did he kill her?"

"Huh?"

"How did Alan kill Nadine? And then how did he kill himself? Gunshot?"

"Oh, no, it wasn't Alan who did the killing. It was Nadine."

"The wife?"

"Yes. Rule Number One in the investigation business, Nicole: never assume anything."

"Well, I—"

"Apparently, Nadine bludgeoned Alan to death with a fireplace poker while he slept, then hung herself with a dog leash."

Nicole couldn't help herself. "Oh, my *God*," she said. Then she quickly straightened up. "Was there a motive? Did she leave a note or anything?"

"Afraid not. We know that she was depressed, so I imagine she just reached a breaking point. It happens."

"Do you think it's connected to the Claire Collins death?"

"Connected? How do you mean?"

"Well, I understand that Nadine called you guys on that one for a wellness check, and now, a week later, here we are."

"Well, sure, that might have sent her over the edge, I suppose. They were good friends, apparently. And I know Nadine's sister died in that car wreck out on Highway 1 earlier this year, too, so that might help explain the depression. But I'm not a psychiatrist, you know. I can't comment on that."

"How did you find out about this one?" Nicole asked.

"Their son Randy called from Cape May, New Jersey. He hadn't heard from them for several days and was concerned. Anyway, that's about all I can really tell you, Nicole. Now I've got a bunch of paperwork to take care of, so if you'll excuse me…"

Detective Barker started walking toward his car, then turned around and added, "Say hey to Walt for me."

***

Paperwork, Barker had told Nicole. He wished that was all it was. In truth, he was heading back to the station to sit Randy and his wife Jill down to tell them of the gruesome discovery. Simon Barker had been a cop for twenty-five years, and though, fortunately, he could count on two hands the number of times he'd had to do it, breaking tragic news was by far the worst part of the job. One never gets used to it or numb to it. Not if they're human, anyway. And even in twenty-five years, he'd never broken the news to a son or daughter that their parents were murder-suicide victims. This was a new one.

Of course he wasn't about to share with Nicole that Randy and Jill were waiting at the station. She was a cute kid and seemed like a hard worker and she even reminded Barker a little of his own daughter, all of which is to say that he didn't mind helping her out when he could. But having her hound the bereaved for a comment that she could publish in the paper? No way. Not on his watch. Barker's duty at this point was to Randy and Jill as much as to anyone else.

Of course the scene at the station was as bad as Barker guessed it would be. Once the patrolman had made the wellness check, discovered the bodies, and called it in, Detective Barker had called Randy and had him go directly to the station, rather than to the Horton's house. He'd come clean on the phone to Randy, telling him his parents were deceased, but he hadn't mentioned the cause or the means. That needed to be done in person. "I'm very sorry, Mr. Horton," he had said. "But we'll discuss everything here at the station when you get here." Then he'd visited the scene while Randy and Jill were en route.

Back at the station, Randy was in utter shock. The color drained from his face when Barker broke the news about the circumstances of the deaths, and it looked for a moment as if he were going to vomit. It took several minutes before he could get his bearings. Barker gave him all the time he needed, but then there was one more tough piece. "I'm going to need you to identify your parents' bodies," he said. "I'm very sorry. I wouldn't ask if it weren't absolutely necessary."

"Yes, of course," Randy replied, with Jill squeezing his hand. "I understand."

By then, the bodies had been removed from the scene and Barker drove the couple to the medical examiner's office, where Randy made the grim identification.

Then he turned to Barker and said, "I'd like to see the house, Detective."

"Well…it's still technically a crime scene," Barker explained.

"Please, Detective Barker. It's very important that I go to the house."

"Okay," Barker nodded. Truth be told, he knew he'd ask for the exact same thing if he were in Randy's shoes. Besides, it wasn't as if Barker had to worry about the scene being compromised. For all intents and purposes, the investigation, save for the formalities, was already over. What was left to discover? Anybody could see what had happened in that house. "I'll drive us there," Barker said, and the three left the station.

Along the way, Randy talked about his mother's depression. "She was getting better," he said. "She'd agreed to see a therapist and it seemed like it was helping. She seemed more herself. Not exactly cheerful, of course, but at least in better spirits. My father said she'd even been going out shopping, finding little trinkets and knick-knacks for the house. We were hopeful. But then came Claire's death. I guess that just sent her over the edge."

"Were you keeping in touch regularly with her?"

"Oh, yes, sir. We talked almost every day. But after Claire's death, she practically wouldn't talk at all."

Jill piped up. "You had said, though, that even before Claire's death, she seemed to be kind of backsliding, remember?"

"Yes," said Randy, thoughtfully. "That's true. The week before, she was short with me on the phone a couple of times. She seemed irritated or something. I didn't take it personally, of course. I imagine there are ups and downs in the grief process."

"Sure, of course," Barker nodded.

Shortly, they pulled up to the house. "You sure you want to go in?" Barker asked.

"I have to, Detective," Randy replied. "I have to see what happened in there."

The three exited the car, strode up the walk past the crime tape, and on into the house. They walked around the downstairs. It looked as if the carpet hadn't been vacuumed in a while. In the kitchen, Madam's dirty paw prints were visible on the floor. Dinner dishes were still in the sink and a tied-up garbage bag was resting next to the back door.

"Nadine never left so much as a dirty spoon in the sink," Jill commented. "She wouldn't go to bed unless the dishes were in the dishwasher and the garbage had been taken out."

"Your parents moved in here when exactly?" Barker asked as he led Jill and Randy out of the kitchen, through the den, and up the stairway to the second floor.

"I guess about twelve years ago," Randy replied. "I had just graduated from college and moved to Cape May."

"So you never lived here."

"That's correct. My childhood home was across town."

"Thank God for that," Jill chimed in. "I mean, it's traumatic enough, you know?"

Barker led them into the master bedroom. Mercifully, the bloody sheets had been pulled off the bed and taken to the crime lab, but the stains had soaked through to the mattress. Randy looked away.

"And then of course, the closet is where we found your mother," Barker said, opening up the walk-in closet door. The leash was gone, but a stepladder rested in the spot where Nadine had apparently used it to tie the leash to a hook halfway up the wall.

"Oh, by the way," Barker said, "there was a dog."

"Yes, 'Madam,'" said Randy. "I forgot all about her. Where is she?"

"One of our officers took her to the vet's on Sycamore. She wasn't doing very well, to be frank. Hungry, dehydrated. Hopefully, she'll be okay."

"Thank you. We'll go check on her." Randy looked about the room, involuntarily shuddered, and said, "Detective, I think I've seen enough. I don't know what I was hoping to see, to be honest. I guess I just couldn't believe it had happened. I still can't believe it. It just doesn't make sense."

"Well, if I can make an observation," Barker said. "I don't know if it will help, but I've been in this business for a long time. Almost as long as you two have been alive. I've seen a lot. The thing is, sometimes, things happen that don't make sense. And they never will. You'll drive yourself nuts trying to make sense of them. Your mother, God rest her soul, was obviously a very troubled woman at the end. Clearly, she wasn't in her right mind. The mistake we often make is trying to attach meaning and sense to acts that are meaningless and senseless. It's a fool's errand, as my father used to say."

Randy nodded. "Thanks, Detective. I suspect you're right. Well, if you could take us back to the station now, we'd appreciate it."

"Of course."

3

"**Y**ou want to do what?"

"An in-depth piece on the Horton crime."
"Nicole, what's to go into depth about?" Walt Massey asked, leaning backward, his chair creaking under the weight. "A woman goes wacko, kills her husband, and then kills herself. We reported it last week. Your article was fine. And plenty deep enough. What else is there to say, really?"

"Walt, you don't find it the least bit interesting that a woman, whom everyone I've talked to said was an absolute gem of a person, decides to kill her husband of thirty-six years—a loving husband from everything I've heard—and then hangs herself with a dog leash?"

Nicole stood in the doorway of Walt's office. The Horton murder-suicide was the perfect feature article, just waiting to be written. How could Walt say no?

"Interesting, Nicole? I don't know if I'd use the word interesting. Morbid, maybe."

"But, Walt, how does something like that happen? How *can* it happen? It doesn't make sense. I think it's worth exploring, don't you?"

"What's to explore? The woman was aggrieved."

"But lots of people become aggrieved. Everyone has to deal with the death of someone at some point. Okay, sure, she was really close to her sister. And the sudden death of her friend didn't help. But murder? Then suicide? There's no reason for it. You saw the toxicology report from Barker. No alcohol, no drugs. She was stone sober. There's a story here, boss."

Walt was quiet for a moment. Maybe Nicole was right. Nadine Horton's actions certainly were mind-boggling. Then again, how many hours was Nicole going to put into this? And would the readers really care?

"Look, Nicole," he said at last, "I'd hate to see you spin your wheels on a story that's probably going to be forgotten the day after we print it. People read the *Gazette* to get the latest on what's happening downtown, which high school team won the big game, what new business opened on Main Street—that sort of thing. Sure, Mrs. Horton's motivations might be of some minor interest, but this ain't *Psychology Today*."

"Oh, come on, Walt. You're underestimating the readers. This whole thing is fascinating. And it won't take much. I've already interviewed half a dozen neighbors in the week since the bodies were found. I found out who Nadine Horton's therapist was, too, so I can interview her. And the Hortons' son is in town taking care of the details of the estate, so I'll get a quote from him.

"Now, look, Nicole, don't go bothering that poor guy. Don't you think he's been through enough?"

"Give me a little credit, Walt. I can be sensitive. I'll just ask him a couple of quick questions and then let him be. Look, I'm just going to write the damn piece anyway, so you might as well just say yes."

Walt sighed. He knew that was probably true. "Promise not to let the rest of your duties slide?"

"I'll work overtime if I have to."

"Yeah?"

"Cross my heart."

"Okay, Nicole. But it better be good."

***

"How did you sleep?"

"Lousy," Randy replied, padding into the kitchen, rubbing his eyes. Jill was already up, sitting at the table having a cup of coffee. The sun had risen, but the sky was gray and it was looking like it was going to be a gloomy New England day. "I can't sleep in this house, Jill."

"I know."

"You can feel it, right?"

"Well, yes, now that you've said something. I've been afraid to mention anything about it because God knows you're stressed enough, but I definitely feel something here. I can't really explain it, though. It's different. It's...weird."

Randy nodded and grabbed a coffee mug. "When we used to visit Mom and Dad here, it was a house of love and...and warmth, you know? Now I dread coming here. It just feels cold and—I don't know—unwelcoming, I guess." He poured his coffee and sat down at the table with Jill. "I've grown to hate these weekends."

"We could stay at a hotel."

"But the expense..."

"Randy, it doesn't matter. We owe it to ourselves, don't you think? It's been hard on both of us."

Randy nodded. "Okay, we'll stay at a hotel tonight."

"Good."

The thought of spending the night away from the site of his parents' gruesome deaths brightened Randy a little. "So, did you make your smoothie this morning yet?" he asked. "If you did, can you save a little for me?"

"I did, and sure. Here." Jill poured some into a glass for him. "I used that ice maker on the counter again. Did you get up and fill it with water this morning?"

"No, why?"

"You didn't? See? This is what I'm talking about. This is what I mean by 'weird.' Randy, I came out here and the ice was already made. It's like the thing came on by itself."

"Are you kidding me? Are you sure you didn't fill it up and just forgot? I mean, we're both living in a bit of a fog these days."

"I'm positive. I didn't touch it."

They both looked at each other and then looked over at the ice maker. Jill glanced back at Randy who seemed to have turned just a little pale.

"*Jesus Christ,*" he said in a low voice. "I'm telling you, Jill, something's wrong with this place. Something is really wrong."

"I know. It just gets stranger all the time. But look, Randy, a few more weekends and we'll have it ready to rent and we won't need to keep coming back here all the time."

"Yeah, I guess."

"And it'll make a wonderful Airbnb. Especially in the summer. And the extra cash won't hurt."

"I know, I know. I suppose we just need to power through the next few weeks."

Randy knew Jill was right about the cash. He'd been passed over for the promotion he was expecting at the bank and living expenses in Cape May weren't getting any cheaper. The inheritance was decent, especially coming on the heels of the sale of the chimney cleaning business. Nevertheless, the rent money would make life just a little easier. Turning the house into a rental property had been Jill's idea, and Randy had to admit it was a smart one. New Liberty, a once quaint New England fishing town, was becoming more and more popular as a tourist destination. Home values were appreciating. The house would make a fine nest egg while, in the meantime, producing a decent income stream. And, should worse ever come to worst, they could always borrow against it.

But there was much work to be done. The obvious first step was getting rid of the bed in the master bedroom, bloody mattress and all. The carpet was pulled up, too. Underneath, the floor was hardwood, but not in very good shape. Rather than refinish it, they'd probably just get new carpet. The room also needed new paint. Randy hated going into the master bedroom. He couldn't stop picturing his father lying in the bed with his skull crushed in and his mother hanging from a hook in the closet. He and Jill slept in the guest room, but he wasn't very comfortable in there, either. Nowhere in the house seemed inviting and Randy couldn't imagine anybody enjoying themselves there. Of course, none of the guests would know what he knew. No one would know that a brutal murder-suicide had taken place under that roof.

For three weekends now, Randy and Jill had made the trek to New Liberty, driving up on Friday afternoon, staying through Sunday, and making trips to the Home Depot in between. It hadn't been just the master bedroom that needed new paint. The whole interior had needed it, too, and much of the exterior. Randy had also done some work on the landscaping and Jill had taken charge of replacing a few key pieces of worn furniture. Most of the personal belongings still needed to be dealt with, and there were a lot of them. Randy envisioned a yard sale and a lot of trips to Goodwill and the Salvation Army.

The very first weekend, they'd brought Madam with them. Madam had been nursed back to health at the vet's, and Randy and Jill had decided to adopt her. But during that weekend, she had hidden herself in the downstairs bathroom and had refused to be cajoled out. Jill had openly wondered at the trauma Madam must have experienced in witnessing the deaths and seeing the dead bodies of her owners. On subsequent weekends, they dropped her off at a boarding kennel.

Also during that first weekend, Jill and Randy had had a visitor. A young woman from the *New Liberty Gazette* was doing a story on mental illness and wanted to ask about the deaths. Jill, not wanting to be rude, had invited her in and they'd sat in the den with the woman glancing around the place and questioning Jill about the circumstances. But Randy had overheard the conversation from upstairs and had come down and politely sent the young woman on her way. The last thing they needed was for the house to be featured in a newspaper article about murder and mental illness.

Now, on this particular morning, Randy and Jill finished their coffees, with Randy committing to tackle the mess in the garage. What was he going to do with all his father's tools? Jill, meanwhile, was going to go through the china cabinet in the dining room. There was a lot of old junk in there, but there were also some pieces that might be worth something. She left the kitchen, walked through the den, and then stopped when she spotted the painting of the two wooden sailboats once again hanging crooked on the wall.

"What's the deal with this thing," she muttered to herself as she straightened the painting for what must have been the tenth time. Such odd things happening. Like that damn ice maker. And on the opposite wall from the picture was a bookshelf with a pair of the most godawful bookends she'd ever seen. There were several books in between, and no matter how tightly she pushed the bookends together, she would invariably discover later that they had somehow slid apart to the point where the books were leaning over. She'd stand the books up straight, push in on the bookends, and go on her way. Sure enough, the books would later be leaning again and the bookends would have moved apart. This incessantly crooked painting was just as infuriating. She didn't dare mention it to Randy. He seemed freaked out enough.

Half an hour into Jill's foray into the overloaded china cabinet, the front doorbell rang. *God, I hope it's not that girl from the paper again*, Jill thought. She opened the door to see a petite woman, probably in her forties, with medium-length dark hair and wearing a conservative business suit.

"Mrs. Horton?" the woman asked.

"Well, yes, I'm *Jill* Horton. Nadine Horton has passed away, I'm afraid. I'm her daughter-in-law."

"Yes, I know," said the woman. "I'm Dr. Kashvi Sharma. I was your mother-in-law's psychologist. I had heard that you and your husband were in town, and I wanted to stop by and offer my condolences."

"Oh, that's very kind of you."

"I've tried stopping in a couple of times over the past week or so, but I seem to keep missing you."

"Oh, yes, well, we're only here on weekends," said Jill. "Please come in. It's so good of you to stop by. Let me get Randy. He's out in the garage, but I know he'd want to meet you. Please, have a seat in the den."

Jill ushered Dr. Sharma into the den and waved her toward the sofa. "I'll be right back," she said, and then she stepped across the room, past the crooked painting, and through the kitchen into the garage, returning a moment later with Randy in tow.

"Dr. Sharma," Randy said, wiping his hands on his pants and striding over to the sofa to shake Dr. Sharma's hand. "It's so nice to meet you. Can we get you anything? Coffee or something?"

"Oh, no, I'm fine, thank you. I won't be staying long; I'm sure you have a lot to do here."

Jill nodded. "You can say that again."

"Listen, Dr. Sharma," Randy said, as he and Jill sat down across from her, "I want you to know that my father spoke very highly of you. He really felt as if you were making a difference. What happened here, well, I don't think anybody could have predicted it. I still haven't quite grasped the whole thing myself."

"Thank you," said Dr. Sharma. "You know, as a trained professional, you like to think you can anticipate anything. But human behavior is complex. I have to confess to you that I'm a little relieved to hear what you just said, Randy. It's not uncommon for bereaved people to look for something, or someone, to blame for the inexplicable. Frankly, I wasn't sure how you'd react to my presence here."

"Oh, Dr. Sharma, we're sure you did your best," Randy assured her. "Obviously, my mother just snapped. Claire's accidental death was clearly the tipping point. But to be honest with you, speaking of blame, it's hard for me not to be angry at my mother, you know? I know it's wrong for me to think like that. I mean, I know she was ill. But I can't seem to help it."

"That's perfectly understandable," Dr. Sharma said. "And very normal. It would be surprising if you didn't feel some anger at your mother. You mustn't beat yourself up over those feelings, and in fact, it's important to acknowledge them."

"Yes, I suppose so."

"Dr. Sharma," Jill interjected, "since you're here, what can you tell us about the last days and weeks of Nadine's life? Randy called her often, but she was very reticent. I'm sure she was much more open with you. As you can imagine, we're pretty curious as to what was going on with her at the end."

"Well, of course, patient confidentiality precludes me from going into details."

"Of course."

"However, I can at least give you some of my impressions. Frankly, she seemed as if she was improving. She was getting out more. And she told me that she was decorating the house."

"Really?" said Randy, thinking of the work he and Jill had been doing. "Decorating?"

"Well, yes, in a manner of speaking. She mentioned picking up a variety of knick-knacks at some consignment shop. Little things that she felt would cheer up the place. It was a good sign. It seemed healthy to me."

"Oh, yes, my father had mentioned the purchases and we've noticed the addition of some things. Some strange choices, frankly. She bought a birdcage, for instance. My parents didn't even have a bird or, as far as I know, any plans to get one."

"And some of it seems like junk," Jill added. "An old lamp, a pair of flameless candles...."

"Well, the choices may seem strange to us," Dr. Sharma said, "but it's clear they were having a positive effect on your mother. Perhaps they were comforting her in some way. She must have felt at least well enough to discontinue our sessions."

"Discontinue?"

"Oh, yes. The last I saw her was two weeks before...well, before her death."

"We didn't realize that," said Randy.

"Yes. So you see, I have no more idea than you what happened in those final two weeks. Of course the death of her friend is the logical explanation, as you've observed. But you have to understand that sometimes the human mind can be very unpredictable. We all want closure when something like this happens. In the end, as unfortunate as it sounds, you might need to resign yourselves to the idea that you will most likely never know what was going through your mother's mind."

"No," said Randy quietly. "I guess we won't."

The three chatted some more until Dr. Sharma mentioned that she had an appointment that she needed to keep. "Again," she said, rising from her chair, "my deepest sympathies."

"Thank you, Dr. Sharma," said Randy, walking her toward the door. "And thanks for coming by personally. It means a lot."

"Of course. And do let me know if there is anything I can ever do for you."

Later that evening, over dinner at a local, casual seafood restaurant, Randy and Jill discussed the meeting with Dr. Sharma. Randy confessed to feeling disappointed. It was nice that she stopped by and he was genuinely grateful for her concern. He knew he had no right to expect anything more from her, but that hadn't stopped him from hoping for an explanation, some insight as to what had possessed his mother, what had compelled her to kill his father and herself.

"I said to Dr. Sharma that Mom must have just snapped as if it's normal for people to do that on occasion. But truthfully, Jill, there has to be more to it, don't you think?"

"Well, you heard her," Jill said. "Human behavior is complex and unpredictable. Sometimes things are...what did she say? Inexplicable, I think was the word." She paused and reached across the table, and took Randy's hand. "We have to try to begin to let this thing go, Randy. I know it's going to take a long time, but we have to start to try."

Randy nodded slowly in reply. "I know."

The two finished their meals in relative silence, passed on the offer for dessert, paid the check, and left. In the car, Randy turned on his phone's GPS app. It was dark and drizzling rain, and he was not altogether familiar with this particular part of New Liberty. He tapped in the address of the hotel they'd checked into late that afternoon and they drove along the main road, both tired from the day's work, neither looking forward to the work that awaited them on Sunday. They'd be boxing up a lot of the personal belongings, including some of those strange purchases. Randy figured he'd take them back to the consignment shop where his mother had bought them.

"I just want to be done with it," he said finally, turning at a traffic light per the GPS instructions. "I want us to be done with this house."

"It won't be that much longer, Randy," Jill said. "A couple more weekends, that's all."

At a stop sign, Randy turned again. "I don't just mean fixing up the place. I don't know, I can't describe it, but I feel like, well, like something is over top of me. Something...dark. It's not just depression. Of course I'm depressed about my parents. Who wouldn't be? But that house, Jill...it feels as if it's some kind of anchor around my neck. Some ghostly anchor."

"Honey, I know. But, honestly, once it's fixed up and we get a steady stream of renters, you'll feel differently. We'll have some money coming in and the house will seem a lot different."

"Maybe."

"Look, you're tired. We're both tired. We'll get a good night's sleep in the hotel and things will look a lot brighter in the morning."

"I suppose you're right," Randy said. Then, forcing a smile, he added, "As usual."

He turned twice more, a left and then, a mile later, a right.

Jill noticed first.

"Randy? Isn't this the road to the house?"

"Huh? No. It couldn't be. It's..." Randy's voice trailed off as he looked around and saw the familiar street.

"Did you put in your parents' address by mistake?"

"No. I put in the hotel's. I'm sure of it."

"Maybe by habit?"

"No way." Randy pulled over and grabbed his phone, looking closely at the screen and double-checking that he'd put the right address into the app. "There," he said, showing the phone to Jill. "See?" Then he shook his head and said, "Modern technology, huh? Stupid thing must have messed up. Okay, let's try this again." He tapped in the hotel address once more. "Okay, now maybe we can get somewhere."

Off they went. It was raining harder now. Randy put the windshield wipers on high but still struggled to see more than a dozen or so yards ahead. The digital voice of the GPS announced the directions. One turn led to the next. Twenty minutes went by. Then, Randy, squinting through the windshield, shuddered at the familiar surroundings before him: his parents' street, their house shortly coming into view.

"Randy?" Jill said, warily. "What's going on?"

"I'll tell you what's going on, Jill," he said in a low, even voice. "Screw Airbnb. What's going on is that first thing tomorrow, we're going to call a Realtor. And then we're going to sell this goddamn house and everything that's in it."

4

*W*ell, *that didn't go so well*, Nicole thought to herself. She'd spent all of ten minutes in the Horton house before Randy Horton had come downstairs and chased her out. She'd tried to explain to Jill Horton, who was nice enough to invite her in, that she was doing a serious piece on mental illness, a piece that, perhaps, could help others.

Nicole decided that maybe the Hortons just needed more time. She'd circle back to them later. And when she did, she'd ask them if they could speak outside. There was no way she was going back into that house. Truthfully, it was a relief when Randy had asked her to leave. The place had a disturbingly eerie vibe. Like nothing Nicole had ever felt before. A feeling of gloom had enveloped her in that living room the moment she'd sat down. She even found herself feeling queasy.

Randy and Jill were obviously trying to clean the home up, but it sure looked like they had a lot of work ahead of them. She didn't envy the effort they'd have to put into it to make the home attractive to potential renters. The living room furniture was okay. Kind of out-of-date, but relatively well taken care of. But so many things out of place. Like the painting on the wall that was askew. Didn't they notice that? And such strange items sitting about. What was with those creepy gargoyle bookends? And the empty birdcage?

The Hortons could wait. Besides, the next stop might prove more fruitful: Nadine's therapist, Dr. Kashvi Sharma. Surely, Dr. Sharma could shed some light on the inner workings of the tortured mind of Nadine Horton. The only problem was it was a weekend and the doctor's office was closed. But, through a little old-fashioned sleuthing—good investigative journalism—Nicole was able to find Dr. Sharma's home address, a condo unit in a four-story building about eight miles outside of town.

The first thing Nicole noticed about the building was the locked entry door, with a keypad for residents and an intercom for guests. She couldn't very well announce herself. Dr. Sharma might decline to let her in. It's the same reason she hadn't called first. It's too easy to dismiss a phone call. When you're standing in front of someone face to face, on the other hand, it's a hell of a lot more difficult for them to turn you down for an interview. She'd learned that in her very first journalism class. Somehow, she'd have to get inside the building and knock directly on the doctor's door.

Nicole waited in her Jeep, pondering her options. Soon, another car pulled up in the parking lot and an older woman with two large paper bags of groceries got out. Nicole sensed her chance. She slid out of her car and began walking toward the door, just like any resident would. Then she turned to the woman.

"Looks like you've got your hands full!" she smiled. "Here, let me help."

"Oh, would you?" said the woman. "That's very kind of you."

Nicole relieved her of one of the bags as the woman punched her passcode into the keypad. She opened the door and Nicole slipped in right behind her.

"Fortunately, I live on the first floor," said the woman.

Nicole followed her down the hallway until they came to the woman's unit.

"I can take it from here," smiled the woman. "Thank you so much!"

"Always happy to help a neighbor," Nicole said, sitting the bag down at the woman's front door. "Have a great day."

"You too."

Then Nicole made for the stairwell at the end of the hall and walked up two flights to the third floor, where Dr. Sharma's unit was located. She smiled to herself at her resourcefulness as she sauntered down the third-floor hallway. Finally, she came to unit 312 and knocked on the door.

Presently, a voice from inside answered, "Yes?" and Nicole could see a shadow under the door.

Nicole drew herself up to the peephole and said, "Dr. Sharma? My name is Nicole Anders. I'm with the *New Liberty Gazette*."

"Yes?"

"Well, Doctor, I'm doing a story on Nadine Horton. You know, the murder-suicide case?"

"How did you get in the front door of the building?"

Nicole forged ahead. "Dr. Sharma, I'm aware that you were Mrs. Horton's psychologist. Would you mind if I came in for a moment? I'd love to ask a few questions."

"I'm sorry, Ms. Anders, but I'm sure you understand the concept of doctor-patient confidentiality. I'm afraid I have nothing I can really tell you."

"Of course, Dr. Sharma, but can you at least speculate as to the reason for Mrs. Horton's actions? Her frame of mind at the time? You see, I'm doing a piece on mental illness and—"

"I'm sorry, miss," Dr. Sharma said and the shadow was gone and Nicole realized that the doctor was no longer standing at the door. She contemplated knocking again and then decided maybe it would be best to leave. A hostile interviewee makes for a poor interview. She'd learned that in her first journalism class, too. Like with Randy and Jill, maybe she could circle back around to Dr. Sharma later.

Two strikes. Well, there was always Detective Barker. He probably wouldn't have much to add, but he was a decent guy and at least he wouldn't throw her out or close a door in her face.

In fact, at the police station, Detective Barker, courteous as always, invited Nicole into his office. "So what can I do for you, Nicole?" he asked taking a seat behind his desk.

"Well, it's about the Horton case, Detective," Nicole said, sitting in the chair across from him.

"I see. Well, I don't really have anything new to tell you. You know as much about it as I do."

"Detective Barker, you've been a cop for how long?"

"Twenty-five years."

"And have you ever seen anything quite like this?"

"Nicole, every crime is unique in its own way. Have I ever seen one this tragic? Well, of course, there have been a few pretty heartbreaking cases that I've had the displeasure of investigating, but, no, I would have to confess to you that this one was especially disturbing. You don't often see something like this, something that comes so out of left field. But crime is often unpredictable. If it wasn't, we'd all do a better job of stopping it, right? Listen, Nicole, I'm not really sure what else I can tell you." Then he paused before adding, "Why don't you tell me what you're look-ing for?"

What *was* Nicole looking for? Truthfully, she didn't know. An answer, she supposed. A reason for why someone would do what Nadine had done. Grief alone? She still had her husband and her son and daughter-in-law. She had a good life. And even if she was despondent enough to commit suicide, why take her husband with her?

"I...I don't know," Nicole answered at last. "I'm just looking for a good story for our readers, I guess." Yes, that was it. Wasn't it?

Detective Barker leaned forward. "Nicole, you're young," he said. "You're at an age where you imag-ine everything in the world makes sense. This has thrown you for a loop. You know what I think? I think you want to make sense of it for yourself, not for any readers of the *Gazette*."

Nicole looked down, breaking eye contact with Barker. She knew he was at least partly right. She hadn't allowed herself to think about it, really. Yes, she wanted to write an amazing piece on the killings, something with her byline that could be a feather in her cap, but at the same time, she couldn't help but wonder in the back of her mind at the pure irrationality of Nadine's act. She wouldn't admit it, but it felt as if Barker had seen right through her.

"Take it from an old guy," Barker continued with a gentle smile. "There's a lot of things in this world that just don't make sense and the sooner you resign yourself to that, the easier things will be for you."

Nicole drew herself up in her chair and adopted a professional countenance, furrowing her brow and looking as serious as she could. "Well, thank you for your time, Detective Barker. I'll be sure to include your observations in the article."

Then she rose and walked out of Barker's office.

Strike three, she thought as she got into her car. She sat for a moment, feeling annoyed by the tears welling up in her eyes. She shook them off and put the Jeep in gear. She had important work to do and there was no time for frivolous thoughts. She was a professional journalist, after all.

5

Lisa Rhodes watched as the electrician put the decorative dome shade back onto her copper table lamp.

"Well," he said, "I can't find anything wrong with it."

"Really? Well...okay," said Lisa. "Like I said, I figured as long as you were here..."

"Sure. It's an interesting lamp, though."

"Yes, isn't it? I found it in a consignment shop."

"Is that a fact?"

"Yes, I think it might be an antique."

"Sure. Could be. The wiring is pretty new, though. And as far as the rest of the house, ma'am, I can't find a single thing wrong. I know it's an older house, but it looks as though it was rewired probably no more than five or ten years ago."

Lisa frowned. "Well, that's good to hear, but how do you explain the lights flickering on and off for no reason? And this lamp seems to burn through bulbs on a weekly basis."

"Honestly, I couldn't say for sure. You called the power company, right?"

"Of course. I called them first."

"Because maybe it's some kind of surge thing."

"Right, but they said it wasn't. They brought a guy out who looked at all the lines coming into the house and tested everything, and he said it was all good. He's the guy who recommended calling an electrician. Said it must be something with the wiring of the house itself."

"And how long have you had these problems again?"

"Just the last week or two. We've lived here about two months. My husband and I just got married."

"Congratulations."

"Thanks. Anyway, when we bought the house, we had a complete inspection. Everything was fine. Then about two weeks ago, these weird problems started. You know, it was just about the time I bought this lamp. That couldn't be it, could it?"

"No, like I said, this lamp is fine."

Lisa was quiet for a moment, finally saying, "Well, is there anything you can suggest?"

The electrician shrugged. "Not really. I've checked everything over, and honestly, ma'am, there's just nothing wrong with it. I'm sorry. You know, maybe it's atmospheric or something. Time of year, dry air..."

His voice trailed off and Lisa could tell he was now grasping at straws.

"Well, thanks for coming," she said, sensing a lost cause. *He probably thinks I'm crazy*, she thought.

"Sure. I still gotta charge you for the trip, you know. Sorry about that. But I'll deduct 10 percent since I didn't really fix anything."

"I understand. Thanks."

After the electrician left, Lisa tried to put the matter out of her mind. With no quantifiable evidence, she would have feared that the intermittent electrical issues were all in her head had it not been for her husband. Ethan was the one who suggested they call the power company in the first place. He was just as annoyed as she was. Of course, electrical work wasn't exactly his forte. If there was going to be any kind of serious work done around the house, it sure wouldn't involve Ethan. His lack of mechanical aptitude was a constant source of amusement for Lisa.

Ethan's talents were in the culinary arts. In fact, the grand opening of the restaurant, his dream practically since childhood, was scheduled for the following week. She had no doubt it would succeed. In all of New Liberty there wasn't one decent casual French bistro. Plus, Ethan had partnered on the restaurant with Darius Young, a longtime friend and a successful entrepreneur in his own right. Ethan knew his way around the kitchen; Darius knew business. Still, it was a gamble. And with the recent purchase of the house? Lisa wondered if the timing was right. Especially since she knew something Ethan didn't know. Something big. Lisa had gone to her doctor's the day before. She was pregnant.

She'd thought hard about it and decided to wait to tell her husband. They had talked about a baby, but hadn't planned on having one just yet. The pregnancy was a total surprise. Lisa thought it might be a little too much to throw at Ethan just now, what with the upcoming grand opening. She decided she would wait until afterward to tell him the news.

He'd take it well, of course. He'd be thrilled. Still, it was definitely going to put some extra pressure on them financially. Fortunately, Lisa had her massage therapist gig and, after being at it full-time for eight years, a steady clientele.

An hour after the electrician left, Ethan came through the front door with his hands full of grocery bags.

"Good God, babe," said Lisa, "did you buy out the whole store?"

Ethan laughed. "There are two more bags in the car. Hey, if we're going to throw a dinner party to celebrate the new house, we're going to do it right. Besides, tonight's menu is going to give everyone a preview of what we're going to serve at the bistro. Now, will you please stop making fun of me and help me with this stuff!? We've got two hours before everybody gets here."

They would need every minute of those two hours. Some of the food had been prepared well beforehand, some of it was still in process when the first guests arrived. Eggplant roulade, duck, bouillabaisse, smoked salmon, snapper, and vegetable Ratatouille were all on the menu, as well as three different desserts, each as rich as the next.

Darius was there with his wife, Vanessa. So were two other couples— Eileen and Darrin Caswell, and Deb and Aaron Hoffman. As Ethan brought out each entrée, he gave a brief description of it. "The secret to the roulade is the fresh dill," he explained.

"Hey, don't be giving too many secrets away," Darius chuckled.

"Well, you don't have to worry about that with me," Eileen said. "You could walk me through the preparation step by step and I'd still find a way to mess it up."

"I can attest to that," Darrin grinned and Eileen gave him a playful poke with her elbow.

"What's the secret with the salmon?" Deb asked. "It's absolutely divine."

"Promise you won't tell anyone?" Ethan said.

"You have my word," Deb replied.

"A little maple syrup."

"No!"

"Yep. But real maple syrup. Not the imitation stuff."

Lisa looked on with pride. It was clear that her husband was loving the reactions of the guests, and he was in his element. This was a man who was born to cook and serve. Maybe the restaurant wasn't such a gamble after all.

After dinner, as Darius was finishing a crème brulee he was splitting with his wife, he seemed to confirm Lisa's thoughts. "Ethan, my brother," he declared, "with this level of food, I'm telling you, we can't lose!"

Ethan smiled. "Man, I sure as hell hope you're right."

Everyone raised their glasses to Darius's comment.

"Here, here!" said Aaron.

Eileen interjected. "Darius is absolutely right, but as delicious as the food is, and as successful as we know the new restaurant's going to be, tonight's about the new *house*. Don't you think it's time you opened your housewarming gifts?"

Lisa looked at the wrapped presents that had been stacked at the end of the table and chuckled. "We said no presents, remember?"

Darrin dismissively waved his hand. "Everyone says that. Nobody means it."

This brought a chuckle from the rest of the room.

"Open ours first," Deb declared. "It's the blue one on top."

"Okay, okay," said Lisa, and soon she was tearing off the wrapping paper. "Oh, I don't believe this," she said laughing when she saw the packaging of the box. "A pair of flameless candles? Really? Funny. Very funny."

The whole table got the joke. Six months before, Lisa had accidentally left a real candle burning in her apartment's living room while she'd gone to take a shower. She came out of the bathroom to the sound of the smoke alarm. The candle had been set near an open window and a breeze had swept the window curtain over top of it. She'd managed to put out the small curtain fire with no further damage done, but not before the fire department had been sent with sirens blaring and lights flashing. There was Lisa in the doorway, wrapped only in a towel, having to explain to the firemen that the danger had passed.

"Well at least you've managed to keep your sense of humor about it," Eileen giggled.

"But seriously, Lisa," said Deb, "I think you'll appreciate these. I know, I know, you're a stickler for the real thing—"

"Occupational hazard," said Lisa. "Mood is half the experience for my massage clients. Real candles, incense, scented oils...no fakery for this girl."

"Well, keep the real stuff for the clients, but use these around the house. These are the ones that flicker and have the auto-timer, too. It always amazes me how real they look."

"Best of all," added Aaron with a sly grin, "you won't burn down this beautiful house."

Laughter mixed with groans followed Aaron's remark, and Deb decided to move the conversation along. "Okay," she said, "that was the joke gift, even though I think they're cool. The next one on the stack is the real one."

The "real" one was a beautiful, personalized stationery set. The other presents followed, a mix of the kind of semi-useful stuff that people rarely buy for themselves and that seem designed specifically to be given as gifts.

Ethan served espresso to anyone who wanted it and the table conversation drifted around to various topics.

At one point, the talk went suddenly silent as the chandelier above the table flickered and then went off for several seconds. Out of the corner of her eye, Lisa noticed that as it did so, the table lamp in the adjacent living room went on. Ethan made a joke about not paying the electric bill, but then the chandelier came back on, the table lamp went off, and the conversation continued. Eventually, the party wound down, and Lisa and Ethan found themselves at the front door waving to everyone as they drove off, having thanked them for their company and their thoughtful gifts.

Back inside the house, Lisa said, "Well, I would say that was a huge success. Everyone had a great time, don't you think?"

"Absolutely. And they really liked the food. Didn't they? I'd hate to think they were all just being kind."

Lisa smiled. "Honey, everything was perfect."

Ethan surveyed the mess in the kitchen and declared that the perfect time to take care of it would be "tomorrow sometime," then grudgingly added, "I guess I'll at least take the garbage to the curb. Those guys always pick up first thing in the morning."

"I'll be upstairs in bed," Lisa said with a coy smile. "Waiting for you." She kissed him on the cheek.

"You won't have to wait long," Ethan grinned, tying up the garbage bag and lugging it out the door.

Lisa glanced into the dining room on her way up the stairs and smiled at the collection of housewarming presents, thinking that before long, she'd have a table full of baby shower gifts. Then she doubled back down to take a closer look at the flameless candles, chuckling to herself. *Very funny*, she thought.

Out in front of the house, Ethan sat the garbage can at the curb and turned to go back in, noticing two candles suddenly appearing in the front window. Apparently, Lisa couldn't resist. *Deb was right*, he mused. *They do look real*. Inside, the living room was empty. Lisa must have hurried up to the bedroom. Ethan locked the front door, turned off the table lamp, and went up the stairs.

———— ◆ ————

The fire department estimated that the blaze had been going strong for probably a full hour before the neighbors were awakened and called 911. By the time the firetrucks arrived, it had become an impossible task to save the home. All that was left was the investigation, the fire marshal's search for the origin of a fire that destroyed a home and took the lives of a young newlywed couple, their bodies found in a poignant embrace in the charred ruins of their upstairs bed.

6

The preliminary fire report was made available to the public a week after the blaze. As a matter of interdepartmental policy, Fire Marshal Brian Stanley had a copy made for the New Liberty police department, even though nothing suspicious had been found. There was no accelerant discovered that would have pointed toward arson, nor, most critically, was there any motive. Ethan and Lisa Rhodes didn't seem to have an enemy in the world.

Detective Simon Barker went to pick up the report in Stanley's office. Walt Massey had been invited to the fire marshal's office at the same time. Stanley knew the public was waiting for his determination as to the fire's cause. The only problem was, he didn't have one. Nevertheless, he knew it was expected that, along with the report, he'd deliver a statement on the investigation.

Brian Stanley, a tall, lean man with salt and pepper hair and mustache, waved his guests into his office. "Have a seat, folks."

Barker came in with Walt following right behind and Nicole in tow. Nicole had insisted on coming along and Walt was grateful to give her another assignment to focus on. She'd been spinning her wheels on that damn murder-suicide, and it was about time she moved on as far as he was concerned. How much more time was she going to waste on that non-story?

Stanley's office in the New Liberty Municipal Center was cramped, as were all the offices in the three-story, nondescript governmental building. It was a strictly utilitarian structure, built in the early 1970s and lacking anything remotely of character. The idea of replacing it with a new building was floated every other year or so, but it never came to pass. Nobody saw any reason to direct tax dollars to the replacement of a building that was still functional. Stanley, for his part, had gotten used to it. He'd been fire marshal for twenty-three years and didn't know anything else. He didn't even mind the noisy window air-conditioning units, which, on this unseasonably cool day, were mercifully shut off.

"Sorry," Stanley said from behind his desk, "I only have the two chairs. If you all want to sit, someone will have to bring a chair in from the hallway."

"I'll get one," Barker said, popping out of the office and bringing in a black, plastic shell chair which he proceeded to plant himself into. Walt pulled out a pad and pen, while Nicole rolled her eyes and turned on the recording app of her smartphone.

"Okay, I'll get right to it," said Stanley, "but first I want to emphasize the preliminary nature of this report. We know it's important to get some information out there, but we do not consider our investigation over. Now, as I told Detective Simon here on the phone, we find no cause to suspect foul play. So, of course that leaves some kind of accidental cause. I can say that we're of the belief that it was not an electrical fire. In fact, I personally interviewed an electrician who was called out to the house the very day of the fire. He had inspected everything and found no problems at all, which was confirmed as well by an earlier home inspection when the couple bought the house just a couple of months prior."

"So why was the electrician called out?" Nicole asked.

"Well, apparently the young woman reported some odd instances of lights going on and off. The electrician didn't find anything amiss. Neither did we. You see, without getting too technical, when you have an electrical fire there are always signs of arcing having affected electrical conductors close to the origin of the blaze. We scoured the scene for such evidence and found none. So that, along with the report from the electrician and the earlier inspection, leads us to believe that maybe the homeowner's complaints of these intermittent problems were, well, for lack of a better explanation, more or less in her head."

Walt nodded while Nicole frowned.

"Nor did we find any evidence of faulty appliances," Stanley continued, "or any malfunctioning gas lines. Further, there was no indication of lit cigarettes, or fire caused by any normal household flammable gases or chemicals."

"Brian, we appreciate what you've ruled out," said Walt, "but what was the *cause*?"

"Well," Stanley hesitated and then said, "at this point, Walt, I can't honestly say that we've found it."

"Is that...normal?" Nicole asked, her brow furrowed. "I mean, in a fire investigation, is it common that there's no cause?"

"Well, now, I didn't say that exactly," replied Stanley. "There's a cause. There's always a cause. Fires don't just start spontaneously. In this particular case, we just haven't yet determined what the specific cause was."

"Can you at least speculate?" Walt asked.

"I don't really like getting into speculation, Walt. About the only thing we know for sure is where the fire started. It seems the curtains in the front bay window of the house were ignited first. The fire spread from there, and, apparently, in an exceedingly rapid manner. Way faster than normal."

"What do you attribute that to?" Walt asked.

"Don't know. Again, there was no accelerant found."

"But if you know where the fire started," Nicole said, "then can't you tell *how* it started? I mean, what would have been responsible for the curtains catching fire?"

"Well, that's just it," said Stanley. "There was nothing in that window that would have caused those curtains to flame. The ledge of the bay window held a flower vase and a pair of flameless candles and nothing more."

"Candles?" Nicole asked.

"Yes, *flameless* candles. Not even turned on."

Barker interjected, "Brian, what about the residents of the house? How come they didn't wake up in time? Were there no smoke alarms?"

"Yeah, that's a bit of a mystery, too. Yes, there were smoke alarms. There was one in the hallway right outside their bedroom, as a matter of fact. All were in working order, and there's no reason to assume they didn't function that night. However, as you know, the couple were found deceased in their bed. The medical examiner says smoke inhalation was the specific cause of death. If there's any blessing to this, it appears that they didn't suffer. But there's no reason they shouldn't have been awakened and been able to get out. The toxicology report mentions some alcohol in his system; none in hers. There's no clear explanation as to how they slept through the sound of an alarm. Or the presence of smoke, for that matter. It's just a damn shame is what it is."

The office was quiet for a moment. Stanley determined it would be a good time to wrap things up. "So anyway, that's where we are, folks," he concluded. "I know you want more answers than what I've given you here today, but I want to assure the town that we're going to continue our investigation until we find the precise cause of the fire. Now, here's the written report; I've made copies for each of you."

Afterward, after everyone had taken a copy of the report and left his office, Fire Marshal Brian Stanley sat at his desk wishing he could believe what he'd said, that they'd find the cause of the blaze. But in twenty-three years, he'd never been so mystified. He knew that Walt and Nicole were going to continue to press him for a conclusion, especially Nicole. She seemed like the persistent type. Eventually, he'd probably have to say that, upon further review, it was determined that it was, indeed, an electrical malfunction. That would work. It was better than the truth, which, from everything Stanley could see, was that this fire had no cause at all.

"And you don't think it's strange?" Nicole was saying. She was riding in Walt's pickup, the two of them heading back to the office after the briefing. "The fire marshal can't determine a cause?"

"You heard him, Nicole; he said he hasn't reached a conclusion yet. It's a preliminary report. Happens all the time."

"I don't know, Walt. I mean, you know Stanley better than I do, but he just seemed kind of baffled to me. He seemed dumbfounded by the whole thing."

"Nicole, you're reading too much into it. Is he frustrated? Sure, who wouldn't be. That doesn't mean he won't solve the problem of the cause of the fire. He is the fire marshal, after all. I'm pretty sure he knows his job."

"But he practically ruled everything out. You heard him. You want to know what I think? That flameless candles had something to do with it."

Walt chuckled. "Nicole, what about 'flameless' don't you get?"

"Laugh if you want to, Walt, but it has to be something, and the candles were in the bay window, right?"

"Flameless candles."

"And, Walt, here's something else to consider. How often have you seen a blaze like this one, a fire that takes out a whole house in the middle of the night?"

"It happens."

"But it's not very common, right?"

"Fortunately, no."

"Okay. So now, let me ask you this: how often have you seen a murder-suicide like the Horton case?"

"Nicole, are you still on *that*?"

"I'm only pointing out the fact that two very uncommon things have happened within weeks of each other and neither one comes with a decent explanation."

"So?"

"So, there has to be a connection."

"A connection? Nicole, how in God's name are the Hortons connected with the couple whose house burned down?"

"I don't know, but it can't just be coincidence. Something strange is going on."

"Look, I'll admit that I can't remember offhand a time when two horrible tragedies like these two cases happened so close together. Or, for that matter, even single cases that were as bad as these. But maybe that just means our town was overdue. Maybe we've been lucky all these years."

Nicole was quiet for a moment. "Yeah, maybe," she said finally. But something didn't sit right. There was a connection. There had to be. Nicole couldn't prove it, but she felt it in her bones.

"Now, when we get to the office," Walt continued, "write up a short article on the fire marshal's report and make sure you stress that the investigation is in the preliminary stages. Then we'll do a follow-up article when we hear from Stanley again."

"Sure, Walt," Nicole nodded, but she wasn't really listening. Her mind was elsewhere.

7

The shell of the house still remained. Most of the walls were intact. Nicole was able to tell which rooms were which, and there were just enough personal effects still recognizable where she could even imagine what the home must have been like before the fire. She stood in what was the living room, the smell of smoke almost overwhelming, and stared at what used to be the front bay window. Of course anything that could have provided evidence had been removed, so the flameless candles were gone. Nicole hadn't expected they'd be there. In truth, she hadn't expected to find anything. There was no good reason for her to be in the house but for some reason she felt compelled to check out the scene for herself.

She turned and looked across the room at the stairway, knowing that it led up to the bedroom where the home's occupants were found. She toyed with the idea of going up, but the stairs were clearly in a bad way and she could easily imagine them collapsing under her weight. She chuckled to herself at the thought of having to call 911 to get herself extricated from a destroyed home that she had trespassed into. Treading carefully, she moved toward the dining room and thought about the accounts from friends of the deceased. They'd been in that very room the night of the blaze enjoying a dinner party. Everyone said how much fun they'd all had. There was enough of the table left where she could almost picture the scene—the laughing, the toasts, the camaraderie. Who in their right minds could have imagined that just hours later the hosts would be dead?

A sharp voice from behind startled Nicole from her reverie.

"Hey! You shouldn't be in here."

Nicole spun around to see a well-built man in a blue uniform. A cop? She looked closer at the badge on his chest and realized he was wearing the station uniform of the New Liberty Fire Department.

"Sorry," she said, "I'm with the *Gazette*. I didn't think anybody would mind. We're working on a story and—"

"Well, it's a scene that's still under investigation," the man said. "Besides that, it's dangerous. That's why it's off limits. You could be arrested for being in here, you know."

Nicole looked into the man's brown eyes and a hint of recognition swept over her. "Donnie?" she said. "Donnie Olson?"

The man looked closer at Nicole and smiled. "Nicole! Geez, I haven't seen you since, well, since graduation, I guess."

"Donnie Olson from New Liberty High School," Nicole declared. "How have you been? I see you're with the fire department now."

"Yep. I joined right out of school. I heard you went away to college."

"University of Connecticut. Journalism. Now I'm with the *Gazette*."

"Well, listen, let's get out of here and talk out front. I didn't mean to yell at you, but you really could get into trouble being in here."

"I understand. Okay, let's go."

Out in front of the house Nicole noticed a red SUV with the New Liberty Fire Department logo on the sides. Donnie had pulled up behind her Wrangler.

"I just happened to be driving by," Donnie explained, "and I saw your car out front. Figured I'd better check it out. Sometimes we get looters, you know."

"Serves me right for not parking out back," Nicole smiled. "But, I must say, there's not much left to loot in this place."

"No, there sure isn't."

"So, Donnie, what do you know about the fire? I've seen the fire marshal's report. In fact, my boss and I met with Officer Stanley. But he labeled the cause as inconclusive, at least for the time being. He seemed pretty baffled, to be honest."

"I'm not sure I'm really supposed to talk about it, Nicole."

"Sure, I understand. But can you at least confirm that the fire started in the bay window?"

"That's what they're saying."

"But how? Stanley said there was nothing there that would have sparked a flame. Just some flameless candles."

"Yeah, I know. But those candles were strange."

"Strange? How so?"

"Stanley didn't tell you?"

"No."

"Well, I probably shouldn't say anything either. I'm sure it will all come out in the final report."

"C'mon, Donnie, for old time's sake?" Nicole coyly smiled and batted her eyebrows. "For a fellow New Liberty Wildcat?"

Donnie grinned. "Well, if you promise not to say where you got this information from."

"Promise."

"Because I could get in trouble."

"You have my word."

"Well, it's really weird. I've seen that pair of candles. They're perfect."

"How do you mean?"

"I mean, it's as though they remained untouched by the fire. They look brand new. They're plastic, and yet there was no melting or anything. Do you know how much heat was in that bay window?"

Nicole shook her head.

"The glass windows exploded, that's how much. But the candles were perfectly intact."

Nicole thought for a moment and then said, "How do you know someone didn't set them there afterward? Maybe an arsonist trying to throw the investigation off track."

"Because I was here that night, Nicole. I was on duty. I helped put out the blaze. Took us most of the night, but we did it. And I distinctly remember seeing those candles in the window. It's funny the things you remember, but I guess I noticed them because my sister has a set like them. Anyway, I went into the house and we did what we could to save the place and I never thought any more about the candles until I read the fire report. And then I saw them in the evidence bin. They're not even singed."

"Well, how do you explain that?"

"That's the thing. It's impossible for them to be that way." Then Donnie's expression turned serious. "Impossible," he repeated. "Don't you see, Nicole? There *is* no explanation.

8

"Where the hell did you get those disgusting things? They're hideous!" Isabella regarded the new additions to the apartment for a moment and then looked at Ashley like she was insane. "What are they anyway?"

"They're bookends," said Ashley. "Duh. Figures you wouldn't know what a bookend is."

"Well excuse me for not recognizing them under those ugly-ass faces."

"They're gargoyles."

"Uh-huh. The one looks like the asshole you went out with last year."

Ashley tried not to laugh. "Yeah, maybe a little," she said, betraying a slight smile.

"What did you pay for them?"

"They were cheap. I got 'em at the same consignment shop where you bought that stupid, useless birdcage."

"Well you're not going to leave them out here are you? In the living room, where everyone can see them?"

"Hell yeah. They're staying right there on the shelf. I don't give a shit what you think of them. Now you and Hana will have a place to keep your textbooks instead of leaving them lying all over the place."

"They're vile, Ashley. Hana will say the same thing. Put them in your room with all the rest of your gothic shit. Maybe we can use them for this year's Halloween party."

"You know, Isabella, your problem is you have shitty taste."

"And your problem is you're a dumb bitch."

"Go screw yourself."

"Bitch."

"Slut."

Then neither one could contain themselves. Both girls started laughing out loud.

Ashley loved her roommates. They'd been the best of friends since junior high and had always shared a unique sense of humor, something only the three of them could appreciate. Over the years, they'd elevated good-natured ribbing practically to an art form. Now they were a month into their third year of coursework at New Liberty College, all of them enrolled in summer classes. This was their first year living together in an apartment. The first two years, they'd lived in the campus dorms. Stepping out into an off-campus apartment had been Ashley's idea. But though they hadn't been living together for long, she'd already learned something about her friends she hadn't really known before. Neither one seemed very concerned about order or cleanliness. "You're both such fucking pigs," Ashley would tell them, and she wasn't kidding. She'd already determined that she'd most likely have to be the one to keep the place neat and tidy.

Worse, Isabella had brought along Wyatt, her African gray parrot. Ashley detested it. It woke the whole apartment up every morning with its whistling and its repetitive "Good morning, Isabella" greeting, which wasn't even cute the first time Ashley heard it, let alone the millionth. It made an absolute mess in the living room with its disgusting habit of flinging peanut shells and feathers onto the floor around its cage. It wasn't even an attractive bird. To Ashley, Wyatt looked like a plucked chicken. Not to mention that she was sure they'd all end up contracting some incurable bird flu. In fact, she'd read online about psittacosis, a disease caused by a bacteria that often infects birds and is transmissible to humans. She'd forwarded a link to both Isabella and Hana. In typical fashion, Isabella had fired back with, "Good. Hopefully, you'll catch it and die and we won't have to listen to you complain about him anymore!" "LOL," Ashley had sent back, and that was all that was ever said about the bird in the apartment.

For Isabella's part, humor aside, she genuinely didn't care for Ashley's taste in décor, nor did she care for her obsessiveness with cleanliness. She was a straight out neat freak, something she hadn't realized before they'd begun to room together. And it was one thing to be obsessed with her and Hana's behavior in the apartment, but did she have to be so obsessed with their personal lives too? Did she have to call Doug Hopkins a loser every single time his name came up? Besides, it wasn't as if Isabella's relationship with Doug was serious. What did Ashley care if Isabella spent time with Doug?

All in all, however, despite the differences, the girls all knew they had each others' backs. They'd been friends for too long. And the humor was a testament to the fact that they could talk to each other as directly as they wanted. There were no secrets between them and no pretenses. They could be as honest as they wanted to be.

Which is why, if Isabella hadn't made her feelings about the bookends clear enough, she was able to take the opportunity to do so again when Hana returned to the apartment from the library while both Isabella and Ashley were still in the living room.

"What's up?" Hana said, tossing her jacket on the sofa, despite Ashley's repeated requests that the girls hang their jackets up.

Isabella replied by picking up one of the gargoyle bookends. "Ashley was just admiring these gorgeous bookends I bought at the consignment shop. Aren't they perfectly lovely? Aren't they just to die for?"

"Bullshit," said Hana, spotting the ruse immediately. "Ashley, with your sucky taste, those *have* to be yours."

Isabella laughed hard.

"You're not keeping them out here in the living room are you?" Hana added.

"Right?" Isabella said, still laughing. "That's what *I* said."

"You guys can both suck it," Ashley said. "You know what? If you hate these bookends so much, you can take them back and exchange them for something else."

"Maybe we will," said Isabella.

"But you'd better come back with something decent or I swear I'm going to torch the next thing you leave lying around here."

"I'll take them back myself," Isabella offered. "Seriously. I've been thinking of going back there anyway. Maybe I can find something with a little more...appeal. *That* shouldn't be hard."

"You know what would be appealing?" said Ashley, "something that would help you slobs organize your shit."

"Oh, here we go," said Hana. "OCD girl wants us to get organized."

"Well, say what you want about these bookends, but at least they're functional. Isabella, maybe you can find something that'll help you guys keep your shit off the floor."

"Yeah, yeah, yeah," said Isabella, chuckling. "Shit off the floor. Got it. In the meantime, I'm out of here."

"Off to Dougie's?" grinned Hana.

"Maybe," Isabella grinned back.

"Back for dinner?" Ashley asked. "I thought I'd make tacos."

"Sure, sounds good."

"Hana?"

"Sure, I'll choke down some of your tacos."

"Oh, I know, let's make blood orange margaritas," Ashley suggested. "Isabella, can you pick up some limes on your way back? We have everything else."

"Will do," said Isabella on her way out the door. "See ya later, bitches."

Ashley smiled. Sure, they could make fun of a couple of bookends. Who cares? There was nothing that could break the bond she'd formed over the years with these two. Absolutely nothing.

Isabella didn't get around to taking the book-ends back to the consignment shop the next day. Or the day after that. Ashley had taken them to her room, unwilling to absorb any more jabs about them, good-natured or not, and so she figured Isabella must have just forgotten about them. Just like Isabella, she thought. Just like she forgot—once again—to clean up after her stupid bird. Just like Hana—once again—left her books lying all over the living room.

Ashley was in the living room surveying the situation, feeling her frustration build, when Isabella came out from her bedroom in her bathrobe.

"Coffee ready?" she yawned. "I've got an early class today."

"No," snapped Ashley. "The fucking coffee isn't ready."

"Whoa, what's gotten into you this morning?" Isabella said, stopping in her tracks.

"Well, what am I supposed to be, the fucking mom around here? Clean the fucking house, cook the fucking meals, make the fucking coffee?"

Isabella knew by the tone and expression that this wasn't one of those times when Ashley was joking around. Something was sure up her ass. *What a bitch*, she thought.

"Ashley, what the fuck? I just asked a simple question. Okay, okay, I'll make the stupid coffee. I just noticed you were up already, so I thought you might have put the coffee on."

Isabella walked past Ashley into the kitchen.

Ashley wasn't done. "And you might want to take a look at your ugly fucking bird. He looks even uglier. His feathers are coming out and he's shitting all over that stupid cage."

Isabella came out from the kitchen and inspected Wyatt, looking suddenly concerned. "Oh, wow, he doesn't look too good," she said softly, poking a finger into the cage. "And he's still not eating."

"Whatever, Isabella. The point is, look at the fucking mess he's making. It's like we're living in a fucking barn. I mean, do you not notice that? You know, it would be one thing if the mess was confined to that godawful cage, but Isabella, look around! Feathers, peanut shells, chewed-up toys—"

"All right!" Isabella shouted. "You don't like the bird. I get it. Do you have to sing this same fucking song every fucking day?!"

"I don't give a shit about the bird one way or the other," Ashley retorted, "I don't like the fucking *mess!*"

"Guys, what the hell's going on out here; I'm trying to sleep."

Isabella and Ashley turned to see Hana in her pajamas.

"Nothing, Hana," Isabella replied. "Ashley's just on the rag again."

"Fuck you, Isabella," said Ashley. "And Hana, what's *your* fucking problem? There isn't a square inch of the sofa that doesn't have your crap all over it. As usual."

"Excuse *me*," said Hana. "I was working late last night on my constitutional law project. It so happens that we have to give presentations this week. I was tired. I was going to pick it all up this morning."

"Oh, I'm sure. Except that you always say that and you never fucking do! Every morning it looks like this."

"Seriously," interjected Isabella. "What is your problem this morning, Ashley? You know what I think? I think maybe you need a boyfriend."

"What, like Doug? The dumb ugly fucking loser? Pass."

Isabella was silent for a moment and then quietly said, "Well, I'm going to get ready for class." She picked up the birdcage and went back into her bedroom.

Hana glared at Ashley for a second, shook her head, and said, "I'm going to try to get back to sleep." Then she turned and disappeared into her room.

Ashley stood by herself in the living room suddenly feeling strangely alone. Obviously, she'd hurt Isabella's feelings. And that look by Hana pierced right through her. But...but so what? Didn't she have a right to be angry with them both? They were fucking slobs and she was sick of it. They didn't even *try* to help her keep the place neat. Nevertheless, it was possible that just *maybe* she'd reacted a little severely. In fact, if she were honest, she'd have to admit that she even surprised herself a little with her outburst that morning. That wasn't like her. That wasn't like her at all. She was easy-going and laid-back. That's what everybody always said about her and what people liked about her. Not only that, these girls were her best friends. Sure, they could be rough with each other, but it always came with humor and from a place of love and respect. That was the very reason they *could* be rough with each other. But what she showed that morning sure didn't come with any humor.

She went into the kitchen and by the time Isabella came out of her room to go to class, Ashley was standing in the living room with a cup of coffee.

"Hey, I made you a cup," she said.

"I'm late," Isabella said tersely, not making eye contact. Then she left the apartment, closing the door behind her and leaving Ashley all alone again.

All was forgotten by that evening. Ashley made dinner again, spaghetti complete with garlic bread. The girls sat around the table and joked with each other like always. The conversation turned serious only once and that was when Isabella confessed that she was in serious danger of flunking her calculus class.

"That shit makes absolutely no sense to me," she said. "And I'm in business management. When, for fuck's sake, would I ever use calculus? I mean, I'm not going to be designing bridges. Derivatives and functions and differentiations—I don't know what any of the shit even means."

"Izzy, don't worry about it," Ashley said. "I aced calculus. If you clean up the dishes, I'll help you with your calc."

"Really?"

"Sure. It's not that hard if you understand the basics."

"Thanks, Ash. You're a pal. Even though your spaghetti is for shit."

"Said the girl who ate an entire plate of it."

"I didn't want to make you feel bad."

The girls all laughed and joked some more as the dinner wound down. Hana mentioned a party that Friday night at one of the fraternity houses and the roommates all agreed that cutting loose at a party was just the thing they needed. As far as they were all concerned, Friday couldn't come fast enough.

***

"Ashley, get out here!" screamed Isabella. "You fucking *killed him!* You stupid fucking bitch!"

Ashley trudged into the living room, still half asleep, finding Isabella sitting on the floor, the birdcage before her, her face red and her eyes big. "What are you yelling about? This is the one morning I don't have class."

"You fucking killed Wyatt!"

"What are you talking about?"

"Wyatt, you twisted bitch! He's dead!"

"He is?"

"Like you don't know!"

"Isabella, I swear, I don't know what you're talking about." Ashley stepped closer to the cage and could see that the bird was lying prostrate, its scrawny legs pointing upward. Isabella slid him out and held his body in her lap and began crying uncontrollably.

Hana padded into the room, rubbing her eyes. "Ashley, what the hell did you do?"

"I didn't do anything," Ashley said.

"She killed him," Isabella said between sobs, staring down at the dead parrot. Then she raised her head and stared hard at Ashley. "You hated Wyatt! You were complaining about him just yesterday, bitching about the 'mess' he made."

"Yeah but, Isabella, I wouldn't kill him!" Ashley looked over at Hana. "*You* believe me, right, Hana?"

Hana didn't say a thing.

"Oh come on, guys," pleaded Ashley. "Sure, I hated the mess, but what do you think I am? Isabella, you said yourself yesterday that it didn't look good. It probably had some kind of bird discase."

"'It' had a name."

"Okay, *Wyatt* didn't look good. Whatever. The point is, you probably needed to take it—take *him*—to a vet."

"He was fine," said Isabella. "I checked on him before I went to bed last night and he was just fine. He had even started eating again."

Nobody said a thing for several moments. Ashley stood in the living room, glancing from roommate to roommate, a slow sense of resentment building within. Who were these people to make such an accusation? Sure, she hated the stupid bird, but for good reason. She wasn't a killer. How could they possibly think so?

She'd be damned if she'd listen to any more of this. It was time to go on the offensive. "He had some kind of bird disease," she repeated at last. "Something *we're* probably going to get now, thank you very much. Isabella, you need to toss his sorry-ass diseased body into the trash out back."

That's all Isabella needed to hear. She'd been waiting for one more hateful comment from Ashley, that evil bitch. She dropped the bird, jumped to her feet, and lunged at Ashley, grabbing her shirt, and shaking her violently. Ashley screamed and pulled Isabella's hair so hard that Isabella released her grip. But then Isabella swung wildly at Ashley, slapping her hard across the mouth. Ashley tasted blood and swung back but her hand was stopped by Hana who had inserted herself between the two.

"Guys, stop!" Hana pleaded, pushing them both apart. "You're going to kill each other! Just stop!"

Isabella, breathing hard, turned away. She retreated to where she'd been sitting, picked up Wyatt, and ran crying into her room.

Hana stared at Ashley, giving her the same look as the morning before. Then she left too. Ashley was left alone again in the living room, putting a finger up to her bloody lip. This time, she didn't feel any remorse.

She couldn't help herself; she felt glad that the stupid fucking bird was dead, the stupid fucking, diseased, filthy bird. She found herself feeling sorry about only one thing: that she didn't kill it herself.

Ashley glanced at her phone: 3 a.m. She lay awake on top of her covers, unable to sleep, listening to the silence of the apartment. She couldn't stop thinking about the events of the day. After being accused of killing Isabella's bird, she'd been quietly raging. She'd gone to her afternoon literary theory class where she sat in her chair and pretended that nothing was wrong. She even met up with a friend at the campus coffee shop afterward, putting on a pleasant face and making small talk. Inside, she was steadily filling with fury.

When she'd returned to the apartment, both her roommates were out. She made a snack and watched TV in the living room until Isabella came home. Then she rose, glared at Isabella, who glared right back, and marched back to her bedroom. That's where she'd been since.

She'd heard Hana come in a couple of hours later. Then she heard them both talking in the living room in hushed voices. About her, no doubt. They'd laugh and Ashley knew they were laughing at her.

First, they accused her of killing the stupid fucking bird, then they laughed at her.

Well. That would be the last they'd ever laugh at Ashley. Stupid bitches.

She sat up and looked around the room. Her curtains were open and the light from the half-moon made eerie shadows on the walls. Her eyes fell upon the silhouetted figures of the gargoyle bookends on her desk. She stood and walked over to the desk and picked one up, feeling its weight in her hand. She could grip it so easily. It fit so perfect in her hand that it was as if it were made just for her. And just for this night.

Such a perfect fit. Such a perfect weight. Then she picked up the second one. Yes, she thought. Yes, these will do nicely. One for each of them. Then she opened her door ever so slowly, being careful not to make a sound. She crept down the hallway, moving noiselessly on the soft carpet, feeling the perfect weight of the bookends in her hands, smiling, feeling the anger already dissipating. It felt so fucking *right*, she thought. Isabella would be first, of course. Then it would be Hana's turn. Stupid bitches.

9

Barker had never seen anything like it. He'd seen plenty of crime scenes before, of course, but nothing like the scene in front of him. It was the evident fury of the act that was so shocking, so disturbing. The young woman's head had been crushed, pulverized. Blood was all over the bed, the floor, the walls. Nothing much was left to provide identification.

And in a second bedroom? The same scene.

Two young women, both brutally, savagely beaten beyond recognition.

Barker took one more look around the room and figured he'd seen enough. Besides, the scene was now seared into his brain and he doubted the sight would ever fade from his memory. The CSI guys would be there soon and he'd happily let them take over. He glanced back at Officer Luke Hawkins, two years on the force, standing in the doorway with his face a greenish-pale tint.

"Hawkins, if you need to get sick, do it in the bathroom," said Barker. "We can't have you contaminate the scene."

"I'll be fine sir," Hawkins managed, before turning and running down the hall.

It was Hawkins, now retching in the bathroom, who had made the discovery. The call had come in from a hysterical, screaming woman. Hawkins and his partner Darnell Turner had arrived to find the woman in the living room, sitting in the corner, her head in her hands, sobbing and shaking uncontrollably. She wore pajamas that were soaked with blood. There was blood on her face and hands. At her feet were a pair of what appeared to be bloody bookends.

The officers had drawn their weapons. "Where's the perpetrator?" Hawkins had said. "Is he still on the premises?"

Turner was about to call for an ambulance, assuming the woman had been stabbed or shot. The blood. There was so much blood. Then the girl managed to mumble, "It was me." She pointed down the hallway and that's when Turner realized she hadn't been stabbed or shot. Hawkins kept his gun drawn and moved down the hallway and soon made the gruesome discoveries.

The girl was still in the living room, curled up against the wall, when Barker came onto the scene twenty minutes later. Turner had tried talking to her, but she'd been incomprehensible.

Now, after seeing the carnage for himself, Barker tried. He knelt down beside her. "Miss," he said gently, "I'm Detective Simon Barker of the New Liberty Police Department. Can you tell me your name?"

The girl took a deep breath and drew her knees up to her body, hugging herself and slowly rocking back and forth. Her eyes were fixed on the floor and eventually she murmured something. Barker couldn't make it out.

"I'm sorry, miss, what was that?"

"Ashley," the girl whispered. "My name is Ashley."

"Okay. And Ashley, can you tell me what happened here?"

"I...I don't really remember. I remember leaving my bedroom..." She paused and began shaking again.

"It's okay, Ashley," Barker said. "Take your time."

A full minute went by. Finally, the young woman continued. "She killed them," she said.

"She? Who's she? Who killed them, Ashley?"

"Ashley killed them," the woman replied. "I saw her do it. She beat their brains out. With those." She nodded her head toward the bookends.

"I see. Okay, Ashley. You sit right there."

Barker rose and walked over to where Turner and Hawkins were standing. Hawkins looked a little less pale-green but not much.

In a low voice, Turner said, "Should we arrest her, Detective Barker? Take her down to the station?"

"Hell no," said Barker. "The girl's out of her mind. Call for an ambulance. Have her transported to Connecticut Institute."

"The mental place?"

"Absolutely. You ride with her and stay with her once you get there. Tell 'em we need a toxicology report pronto. I'll meet you there and we'll make the formal arrest. In the meantime, what have you found on the victims?"

"We found their IDs," Turner replied. "Isabella Garcia and Hana Lin. Students at the college. This one," Turner said, pointing an elbow at the young woman rocking herself on the floor, "is Ashley Mills. She's a student too."

"Young women with their whole lives in front of them," Barker said, shaking his head.

"What do you suppose got into her?" Hawkins asked.

"Who knows? She just snapped, I guess." But even as Barker said it, in his most even, rational, professional voice, he didn't believe it. People snap, sure. But this was more than that. This was an otherwise normal college girl who went on a stark-raving-mad killing spree, the bloodiest Detective Simon Barker had ever seen.

"Search the place for drugs," he added. But somehow he knew that wasn't it either. Acid? PCP? The most paranoid-inducing, hallucinatory chemicals available on the street couldn't explain this level of violence. Besides, Ashley sure wasn't showing any violent tendencies now. Plus, here it was just a little after 4 a.m. Everybody had presumably been in bed. The apartment clearly hadn't been the site of a party. So did Ashley just decide to get up in the middle of the night and snort something infused with PCP by herself? That seemed hardly likely.

"I'll be out front waiting for the CSI guys," Barker said. He nodded at the officers and strode out the front door, maintaining his composure and professionalism until he'd closed the door after him. Then he walked around the side of the apartment building and retched himself.

The preliminary toxicology report was negative, which Barker learned when he got to Connecticut Institute after having spent an hour with the CSI squad in the students' apartment. The sun was just starting to rise by then. Ashley had been checked in, cleaned up, and put into a hospital gown. Officer Turner had remained by the door of the room she'd been taken to, but upon Barker's arrival, and at his insistence, a doctor and an orderly brought Ashley to a separate room where Barker could question her.

"Go easy on her," the doctor said as the orderly rolled Ashley into the room in a wheelchair and positioned her across from where Barker was seated. "Obviously, she's been traumatized. Please keep your questions short."

Barker nodded, and, for the first time, got a good glimpse of Ashley. She was attractive in a kind of all-American way. Blonde, blue eyes. The girl next door. The exact sort of person you'd never, in a million years, associate with such a brutal crime.

"Ashley, I'm Detective Simon Barker of the New Liberty Police Force. We met in your apartment. Do you remember?"

Ashley was staring at the floor but nodded slightly.

"It's my duty," Barker continued, "to inform you at this time that you're under arrest for suspicion of murder. Do you understand?"

Ashley nodded again.

"Further, I need to tell you that you have the right to remain silent and you have the right to retain counsel. Do you understand this? Would you like to have an attorney present?"

Ashley shook her head. "I don't need an attorney," she said softly.

"Okay then. Ashley, for the record, can you tell me what happened in your apartment?"

Ashley looked up and, with a blank face and cold eyes said, flatly, "I killed them."

Barker realized that whatever emotion the girl might have had, the horror of the murders had drained it all out of her. There was nothing left behind the eyes of the girl and he felt as if he were talking to a zombie. "Can you tell me why?" he continued. "Can you tell me why you killed them?"

Ashley was quiet for several long seconds. Barker was about to repeat the question, believing that maybe she hadn't heard it, when she finally answered. "I don't know."

"You don't know?"

"No. I just did it." Ashley spoke in a monotone that Barker found vaguely disturbing. What she said next didn't do very much to dispel the feeling. "I loved them. They were my best friends. But then I killed them. With the bookends. One for each of them. I smashed their skulls. I could hear the skulls breaking as I did it. But I couldn't stop. First Isabella and then Hana."

"I see." Barker took a deep breath. "And you don't know the reason?"

"No. I just had to kill them. I had to break their skulls. The bookends were right there. The bookends. One for each of them. I had to kill them. Do you see?"

"Detective Barker," the doctor interjected. "I'm afraid I have to insist that we take the patient back to her room now. I trust you have everything you need."

Barker couldn't imagine he was going to get anything more out of Ashley that might actually be of use. "Yes, doctor. Naturally, I'll need to keep my officer here."

"I understand."

"I'll be in touch with you later today to make arrangements to have her transported to county. When you think she's ready to be transported, of course."

The doctor nodded to the orderly who wheeled Ashley out of the room and down the hallway with the doctor following along.

Outside in the hallway was Turner. "I'm going to the station," Barker told him. "I'll send someone to relieve you ASAP."

"Thanks, Detective Barker," Turner said. "Hey, what went on in there? What did she say?"

"She said she had to kill her roommates. No reason given."

"She had to?"

"She had to."

Then Barker turned and walked through the lobby and out into the sunshine of a new day, never in his life feeling so glad to be leaving a hospital.

10

I t was not easy to set up an interview with Ashley. Prisoners in Bridgeport Correctional Center, a level 4 high-security prison, have to fill out a request to enable a particular person to visit them. The request has to be approved and for visitors outside of immediate family, the approval is at the discretion of the warden. So Nicole needed Ashley's cooperation first, and then she needed the warden to okay the visitation of a reporter. Media access to prisoners is never guaranteed.

But to get to Ashley, Nicole needed to go through her attorney. Ashley's parents had spared no expense and had hired Isaac Thornton, a virtual celebrity in the area. Tall, fifties, with wire-rimmed glasses and always dressed in a custom-tailored Gucci suit, Thornton had successfully defended dozens of high-profile clients from a wide variety of charges. Nicole had tried to interview him at the arraignment two days after Ashley's arrest, but got no more than a terse "no comment" from him as he exited the courthouse. Ashley had been in no condition to be present herself and Thornton had entered a plea of "not guilty" on her behalf. Detective Simon Barker had announced the day before that Ashley had admitted to the killings and so the entire town was curious as to what Thorton's strategy was. Most thought he'd eventually amend Ashley's plea to not guilty by reason of insanity.

It was two weeks after the arraignment before Ashley was finally transferred from Connecticut Institute to Bridgeport Correctional. Access to her at Connecticut Institute had been impossible. Visitation was limited strictly to immediate family. Nicole had to bide her time until Ashley had arrived at the prison where, due to the horrific nature of the crime, she would be held without bail until the trial.

After the transfer, Nicole spent another week trying unsuccessfully to get in touch with Thorton, hoping he would agree to advise his client to speak to the media, perhaps to elicit sympathy. When he finally returned Nicole's calls, it was to tell her that he unequivocally would not allow his client to be interviewed by Nicole or by any member of the media.

The conversation was short and after it ended, Nicole sat at her desk in the office of the *New Liberty Gazette* pondering her next steps. Without a statement from the killer herself, the article was going to be incomplete.

Walt came out of his office pondering the question of why Nicole was pondering.

"Seriously," he said to her, having overheard her conversation with Thornton, "what did you hope to gain, Nicole? Assuming Thornton would ever give you permission to talk to the girl, what do you think she'd tell you?"

"The reason, Walt. Why she did it. Aren't you curious?"

"No. I know why she did it. She went loco."

"Damn it, Walt, you said the same thing about Nadine Horton! You know, you must be the least curious journalist in the history of journalism."

"Ah, there's your problem, Nicole. You see?"

"No."

"I'm not a journalist. I'm a businessman. And the *Gazette* is a business. And, I might add, a paper with a reputation for printing decent, wholesome, community news. We're not a tabloid. You have to admit, Nicole, that your ideas lately have bordered on sensationalism."

"Community news, Walt? What's more newsworthy to this community than what's gone on around here over the last three months? An unpredictable murder-suicide, a mysterious house blaze that left two people dead, and the out-of-left-field brutal killing of two young women by their roommate."

"There you go trying to make a connection again."

"Walt, how are they *not* connected?!"

"They're just not, Nicole. Shit happens. We've been over this. These are all terrible tragedies, but terrible tragedies happen."

"Bullshit. There's more to all of this. There has to be."

"Like what?"

Nicole was quiet for a moment. "I don't know," she said at last. "But there's a connection. And I'm going to find it."

Walt sighed. "Okay, fine. But find it on your own time. Yesterday I asked you to write something up on the Fourth of July festivities. Did you call Mr. Freeman like I'd asked you to? To get a quote about this year's high school marching band? Did you talk to the mayor about the fireworks display? Where's my article, Nicole? Huh? Where?"

Fourth of July festivities? Marching bands? Why couldn't Walt see the universal appeal of the story that was right under their noses? Nicole had had enough. At her wit's end, she rose from her desk and exclaimed, "You know what, Walt? Write your own damn article! You want a quote for your stupid little paper about the goddamned Fourth of July? Here's a quote: stick the mayor *and* his fireworks display up your ass!"

Nicole slammed the door to the office so hard on her way out that Walt was surprised the glass didn't break. Then he heard the squeal of her tires as she sped down the street.

Walt sat at his desk, taken aback by the outburst. What had gotten into her? Well, he had to admit, though he never would to her, that it *was* a strange chain of events that had befallen New Liberty. The truth was, it had unnerved him, too.

It had unnerved the whole town. Everyone was talking about the deaths, mostly in hushed tones. In the grocery store, at the coffee shop, across back-yard fences. The town had never experienced such a run of tragedy. You could feel a palpable sense of unease wherever you went. But in Walt's view, that's exactly why the paper needed to focus on things like the Fourth of July festivities. In these times, people needed to see the lighter side of life around New Liberty. They wanted happy news sto-ries that were positive and uplifting. Nicole, she was young. She didn't understand. She was full of spunk and enthusiasm and imagination. After you reach a certain age and you become comfortable with a certain way of living, you don't go looking for things that are going to upset the apple cart. People need stability. Security. Life needs to make sense. These deaths didn't make any sense and nev-er would. Why write about them? Why harp on them? And who in their right minds would want to read such morbid stuff?

Walt knew that Nicole would come back. She'd apologize for her outburst and he'd accept it. She'd learn. She'd come to understand what was really important and she'd give up on this idea that the deaths were somehow related. Maybe they could compromise. Maybe she could write some sort of cathartic piece about how the town was handling the tragedies. Interview shop owners and people on the street. Something positive, something healing. That would be much better than interviewing people like Ashley to try to make sense of the nonsensical.

But there would be no getting around it: Nicole had to understand who was the boss. She had to learn that you can't talk to a superior like that. He'd suggest the article about the effects of the deaths on the town, but first, damn it, she was going to write that piece on the Fourth of July!

Like she always did whenever life got her down, Nicole went to her sister's house. Kelly was older by three years, but seemed even older. She was wise and mature and exuded a sense of life experience beyond her years. "An old soul," their mother was always fond of saying about Kelly.

Kelly made lattes that afternoon and listened patiently to Nicole rant about her job and her boss and then gave her opinion succinctly, as always.

"Do you have another job lined up?" she asked.

"No," Nicole replied. "I mean, I haven't looked around. I—"

"Do you need the money?"

"Well...yes."

"Then you'd better go back and apologize, Nick. And while you're writing about Mr. Freeman and the high school band, you can start looking for a job elsewhere. Until then, you've got no choice, it seems to me."

Of course Nicole knew Kelly was right. She'd have to return to Walt and the *Gazette* and write about the inane goings-on of their small town. But that, it seemed to her, didn't make her wrong about what she felt was a major news story being buried.

"You see it, though, right?" she said to Kelly. "I mean, the series of these incidents in this town is just too bizarre to believe."

"Well, they're bizarre, sure. But, Nicole, how could they be connected? You know what I think? I think you want them to be connected, not for the sake of a story, but because it would be comforting to know that life isn't this random. But it is, Nicole. Random things happen all the time. Not everything has a reason."

Nicole chuckled. "Funny," she said, "that's just what Detective Barker told me. Everybody seems to know my motivation for digging deeper into these cases but me. Everyone's a psychologist, I guess. Well, maybe all of you are right. But maybe, just maybe, you're all wrong. Can I tell you a secret?"

"Of course."

"I mean it; this cannot leave this room. I made a promise."

"I won't tell a soul."

"Well, remember Donnie Olson?"

"Vaguely."

"He was in my class at New Liberty."

"Okay."

"Anyway, he's with the fire department now. I ran into him at the house where the fire was. And you know what he told me? He told me that they have no idea how the fire started, but they know that it started in the front bay window where a couple of flameless candles sat. You know, like the kind we have? But there was nothing else there. And here's the kicker: the flameless candles came through the blaze completely unscathed. The heat was enough to shatter the windows, but the candles were in perfect shape. Now, how do you explain that?"

Kelly shrugged. "I'm sure there's an explanation, Nicky."

"An explanation of how something made of plastic can look brand new after it's been exposed to flames the severity of which were enough to burn down a house?"

"So what are you saying?"

"Well, I'm saying...I'm saying..." Nicole paused. What *was* she saying? "I don't know, Kelly. I guess I'm just saying that there's more to these tragedies than meets the eye. And I can't believe that people wouldn't be interested in reading more about them, about how they're linked. And, well, it wouldn't do my career any harm to have a piece published on such a serious matter. I mean, that's what journalism is all about, you know?"

Kelly nodded. "You'll get your chance, Nicole. You have to be patient. And who knows, maybe old Walt will see it your way. But not if you're screaming at him and storming out of the office."

"I know, I know," Nicole sighed.

The two chatted some more, the conversation eventually turning to more mundane, family matters, and then they said their goodbyes.

"Thanks for listening, big sister," Nicole said on her way out the door.

"Anytime."

Then Nicole started the drive back to the office to reclaim her job. But her earlier mention of Detective Barker got her thinking more about the roommates' murders. She'd read the arrest report, but had she missed something? Wouldn't hurt to double-check it and maybe get another comment from Barker on the matter. After all, he'd had a few weeks to think about the murders. Did he have anything fresh to add? It was worth a shot.

Nicole took a slight detour and stopped off at the police station.

"Nicole, you're always welcome to stop by," Barker told her from behind his desk, "but like I said the other day, and the day before that, and three days before that, I have nothing new to report. Sorry. You know everything we know."

Well, so much for that idea. Nicole turned to go, then thought of something and stopped. "The arrest report mentioned the murder weapons," she said.

"Yes?"

"Bookends."

"That's right."

"Kind of odd, no?"

"Not really. There were no guns or butcher knives in the house. In the heat of the moment, people grab what's close by."

"Where are the bookends, Detective Barker?"

"In the evidence room."

"Can I see them?"

"Why?"

"I don't know. I just think it might be important somehow."

Barker sighed. The quicker he could show Nicole the bookends, the quicker she'd leave. "Okay, follow me. But then I really have to get back to work, Nicole."

"I understand."

In the evidence room, Barker told Nicole to wait behind the counter while he went back to a shelf and retrieved two plastic bags, each containing one of the bookends. He came back up to the front of the room and set them on the counter.

"One for each of them," he said, frowning.

"Huh?"

"That's what Ashley kept saying. 'One for each of them.' Talked about their skulls breaking." Barker shook his head. "Good Lord, what a sick, sick kid."

"But that's just it, Detective. She wasn't sick. At least not until that night. You noted it all yourself in the police report: valedictorian at her high school, student council president, tons of friends on social media. The day before the killings she was posting about a fraternity party she was planning on going to. *With* her roommates."

"Nicole, you never know what secrets people are keeping inside of themselves. Anyway, here are the bookends, okay? Now that you've seen them, I really need to put them back."

Nicole's mind started to swim. "Wait," she said, looking closer at the gargoyle figures. "I've seen these before!"

"These?"

"Yes! I could never forget them. They're so damned creepy. The Horton house. When I stopped by to interview Randy and Jill Horton. They were there, detective. Those same bookends. They were there!"

11

Paul Dixon stood back and looked at the oil painting. Dixon was no expert in art, but he knew what he liked, and the painting of the two wooden sailboats in the consignment shop was exactly that. A sailor himself, he liked the way the boats were depicted—racing against each other, sails full, both heeling over. Sailing, Paul knew, was the perfect mix of form and function, something, in Paul's estimation, that the artist had captured beautifully.

Shortly, Paul's wife Doreen came into the shop with their three children following right behind her—Samantha, Kristin, and Cameron. Paul scarcely noticed when the little bell above the door jingled, but Cameron, the youngest at six years of age, got his father's attention by announcing, "Dad, you promised we'd get ice cream!"

"Huh?" Paul looked up from the painting to see his family looking at him expectantly. "Oh, sure, Cameron. The ice cream shop is right next door. Daddy's going to buy this painting first." Then he turned to Doreen, holding up the painting and grinning. "So what do you think?"

Doreen smiled and shook her head. "Why do you always wander in here whenever we come downtown?" she asked, sidling up to her husband.

"I don't know. They always have something interesting. Like this painting. I don't remember seeing it here before. Seriously, what do you think? Pretty cool, huh?"

"Sure, I guess," Doreen said, her brow furrowed. "Looks old."

"Sure. It's probably an antique."

"Where would we put it?"

Paul sensed his wife's misgivings. "Don't worry, it'll go in my office in the basement."

"Oh, well, in that case, I love it!"

They both laughed and Paul leaned over and gave his wife a quick kiss on the cheek. "Okay, I'll go pay for this. Meanwhile, why don't you take the kids next door and I'll catch up."

"Sure. Want me to order you something?"

"Just a small cone. Rocky road, I guess."

"Rocky road it shall be," said Doreen. "Come on, kids. Ice cream!"

"Yay!" Cameron exclaimed.

Paul grabbed the painting and made for the counter as Doreen and the children left the shop.

"Nice, isn't it?" he said to the girl at the cash register, laying the painting carefully across the counter.

"Sure," she replied, taking Paul's credit card. "You know, it's actually the second time we've had it in here. Someone bought it and then just a month or so later it was returned."

"Really? Wow, why would anyone return this?"

"Who knows? Maybe they sold their house and moved away or something. We get a lot of stuff in here whenever people move. Or downsize. Do you want me to wrap some packing paper around it?"

"Would you?"

"Of course."

Paul paid for the painting, put it into the trunk of his car, then met the rest of his family in the ice cream shop. Afterward, they took a stroll through the downtown park and then the Dixon family made it back to their split-level ranch home where Paul headed straight for his basement office with his new purchase. He regarded the wall above his desk for a minute or so and finally decided that to make room, the diplomas could come down as well as a couple of the old pictures of his family growing up—photos of his mother and father and his brother Brad. Brad was younger by ten years, an almost insurmountable gap when they were young, but as Brad made it into his teen years, Paul became a caring mentor and the two grew close. Now at twenty-six, Brad still thought of Paul as his trusted confidante. He counted on the benefit of his older brother's experience, especially about family matters now that Brad had a child of his own.

Paul removed the diplomas and family pictures and stacked them on his desk. He looked around considering the options of where they could be rehung, but decided he would figure that out later. Then he set about hanging the old oil painting of the sailboats. He couldn't wait to show it to Brad. The two had sailed together for years. Paul had learned sailing from their father and had, in turn, taught his little brother. They had always had a boat growing up. It was a natural part of their childhood.

Now, Paul's own boat was sitting at the dock behind the house. The ranch home rested on a canal that led out to the sound, and tied to the dock was Paul's pride and joy: *The Wanderer*, a thirty-three-foot Catalina sloop. It was a good length. Big enough for a decently sized cabin, but not too big to where Paul needed extra hands. He was quite comfortable with taking *The Wanderer* out by himself and did so often.

The next day was the Fourth of July and Paul was toying with the idea of taking *The Wanderer* to Half Moon Island, a half-day's sail across Long Island Sound and a half-day's sail back again. His plan was to ask Brad later that evening to accompany him. He and Doreen had invited Brad and his wife Brooke to come over with their eight-month-old baby, Emma, offering to throw some burgers on the grill. Probably, Brad would beg off from sailing, citing the need to spend the day with Brooke and Emma, but that was the exact reason Paul wanted to invite him. With the new baby, it had been months since the two brothers had spent any quality time together. Doreen understood. He'd already asked her. She only made him promise to be back in plenty of time to take everybody downtown for the fireworks display.

With the picture hung, Paul went upstairs but couldn't resist returning just fifteen minutes later to take another peek at the painting. He noticed it was slightly askew and realized that he must not have properly centered it on the hook. That correction made, he stood back and admired the boats once more before turning off the light and going back upstairs.

***

With Paul and Doreen's kids playing on a slip-and-slide in the backyard, the adults sat on the deck chatting and enjoying the summer evening. Paul and Brad were each holding a beer, Doreen held a glass of chardonnay, and Brooke was holding a sleeping Emma.

"Excellent dinner, guys," Brad remarked. "Paul, you're a regular Bobby Flay with that grill."

"Yes," agreed Brooke, "but it was Doreen's pasta salad that tied it all together."

"Well, we appreciate having you here," smiled Doreen. "Emma's getting cuter every time I see her. God, it seems like just yesterday that mine were that small!"

Paul turned to Brad with a sly grin. "So guess where I'm going tomorrow, little brother?"

"Let me take a wild stab," Brad chuckled. "Half Moon Island?"

"You betcha!"

"That's become quite a Fourth of July tradition for you, hasn't it?" Brad smiled.

"Yep, it really has. Sorry you missed it last year."

"Yeah, let's see, I was in Chicago at that convention. Thank God I'm not having to travel as much these days with my new position."

"Yes," Brooke added, "especially with our little one."

"So what about coming along this year?" Paul asked. "Just you and me and *The Wanderer*. What do you say?"

"I don't know, Paul," Brad said glancing over at his wife. "I hate to leave Brooke alone all day, what with the baby and all. You know how it is."

"It's okay, Brad," said Brooke with a grin. It didn't take mindreading skills for her to grasp her husband's wish to accept the invitation.

Brad brightened up. "Really, babe?"

"Well, I know how much you guys like to get together and sail. And you've been so good with Emma. I'd say you deserve a little time with your brother. But Paul, you'll have him home by dinner, won't you?"

"Oh, for sure," Paul replied. "I figured we'd all get together tomorrow evening for the fireworks."

"Oh, that would be nice," said Brooke.

"Hey, Dad, can we come sailing too?" Paul turned to see that ten-year-old Samantha had left the slip-and-slide and made her way to the deck. Kristin and Cameron soon followed their big sister.

"Yeah, Dad," said Kristin. "Can we come?"

Doreen bailed her husband out. "This trip is just for your dad and your uncle," she said. "But Dad's going to take you all out soon, aren't you, dear?"

"I promise," Paul said. "How about next weekend we all go out for the day? In the meantime, Uncle Brad and I will be back in time for the fireworks show tomorrow evening. How does that sound?"

"Yay, fireworks!" Cameron shouted.

"Aw, but I want to sail to Half Moon Island tomorrow," Samantha insisted. "I want to go sailing!"

"I know you do, honey," said Paul, "but this trip is just for your uncle and me. Next weekend, huh? I'll even let you take the wheel."

"Me too?" said Kristin.

"Sure, everybody will get a chance to take the wheel. We'll go out all day. We'll bring snacks and everything."

That seemed to satisfy the kids and back they went to the slip-and-slide.

"Now, listen," Brooke said, leaning in toward her husband and brother-in-law, "you guys be careful tomorrow, okay?"

"No worries," Paul replied. "The marine forecast says no greater than ten to fifteen knot winds, a light chop on the water, and zero chance of rain. You couldn't ask for a better day."

"We've certainly been out in worse," Brad laughed. "Remember that time when that storm blew up out of nowhere?"

Paul laughed, too. "Oh, man, we couldn't get the sails down fast enough. That old boat held together, though, I'll say that much. I don't know how Dad did it, but he managed to keep that thing patched up somehow. Damn, that boat was older than Grandpa."

The two reminisced some more about their lifetime experiences of sailing, eventually stopping when they noticed the girls were looking a bit bored by the conversation. Brooke sure was a good sport, though, Paul thought. Letting Brad go sailing with him to Half Moon Island? This was going to be great!

"I'm heading in to grab another beer," Paul said. "Anybody want anything?"

"Yeah, I guess I'll take just one more," Brad replied. Then he looked over at Brooke who gave just the slightest trace of a scowl. "On second thought," he said, "I guess that's it for me tonight."

Paul chuckled to himself and went in through the back door to the kitchen. He grabbed a beer out of the fridge then, on a whim, decided to jog down the basement steps to take a quick look at the new painting. He'd shown it to Brad earlier and he'd loved it.

He flipped on the light and glanced at the wall above his desk. *Damn*, he thought. *It's crooked again.* He straightened it, smiled, and then went back up the stairs to rejoin the others out on the deck.

The next morning, Paul rose early, packed things up, and headed down to *The Wanderer* to get her rigged and ready in anticipation of Brad's arrival. He never made it back down to the basement. Had he taken a look above his desk that morning, he would have seen, to his annoyance, that the painting of the two wooden sailboats, racing against each other, sails full, both heeling over, was crooked once again.

12

The morning was clear and warm. Temperatures were expected to be in the low eighties by the afternoon. There was a light breeze coming onto the dock as Paul and Brad loaded the cooler onto the boat.

"Perfect day," Brad remarked.

"I know," Paul agreed. "Clear skies all day. Marine forecast said something about possible thunderstorms east, but they're talking way east, like beyond Block Island."

"What's that about thunderstorms?"

Paul turned to see Doreen walking toward the dock with a can of sunscreen spray.

Paul grinned and winked at his brother. "I was just telling Brad that the one thing they're *not* expecting today is thunderstorms."

"Uh-huh," Doreen said with a trace of skepticism. "Well, there'd better *not* be thunderstorms."

"It's going to be beautiful all day, honey," Paul assured her. "Perfect sailing weather."

Doreen sighed. "If you say so. Here, you forgot the new can of sunscreen. We ran out last time, remember?"

"Oh, thanks."

Samantha, Kristin, and Cameron were out in the yard buzzing about.

"Daddy, I want to go sailing!" said Samantha. "Can't I come with you?"

"Me too!" said Kristin.

Little Cameron was normally one to parrot his sisters but remained quiet for the time being.

"Now, come on, kids," Paul replied, "we talked about us all going sailing next week, remember? We'll go way far out, I promise. And don't forget, your uncle and I are going to be back in plenty of time for us to go downtown and watch the fireworks this evening. That'll be fun, right?"

"I guess so," Samantha said.

"I guess so," Kristin repeated.

Cameron stayed silent.

"Sure it will," said Paul. "It'll be great." The kids went running off and Paul turned to Doreen. "What's the matter with Cameron this morning? He seems unusually quiet."

"I know, I noticed that too. I hope he's not getting sick. He'll be devastated if he has to miss the fireworks tonight. I'll keep an eye on him."

Meanwhile, Brad had removed and stowed the mainsail cover, attached the main halyard, and fired up the diesel engine. "Hey, what are we waiting for?" he smiled. "She's all ready."

As the kids gathered back at the dock with Doreen, Brad tossed the dock lines and Paul began maneuvering into the canal that would lead them out to open water.

"Have fun!" Doreen shouted.

Paul and Brad smiled and waved and before long the dock was out of sight. Entering the Sound, they cut the engine, raised the main and unfurled the jib. The breeze caught the sails and *The Wanderer* clipped along smoothly through the light chop.

"The wind is in our favor," said Paul behind the wheel. "We can sail a straight shot to Half-Moon Island."

In fact, the normally three-hour trip to the island took only two and a half. The brothers anchored in a small inlet, ate sandwiches that Doreen had prepared, and had a couple of beers. But on the way back, the wind shifted. It blew straight from their destination, forcing them to take a zig-zag course as they beat against it.

"Gonna take a little longer getting back," Paul said.

"So what?" said Brad. "We made good time going out. We'll still be back at the dock in plenty of time.

Or, worse comes to worst, we can always fire up the motor."

"Bite your tongue! This is a sailboat, not a motorboat!"

Brad laughed. "Right you are, brother. We'll do it by sail. Of course, it might require another beer."

"I was thinking the same thing. Grab me one too, would ya?"

The brothers sailed another hour before Paul noticed a change in the sky over his shoulder. "Not sure I like the looks of those clouds," he said to Brad.

Brad looked to the east where the puffy white clouds from earlier had grown bigger and darker. On the horizon the clouds reached down to the sea.

"It's raining over there for sure," said Brad. "What do you figure, about ten miles?"

"And coming this way," Paul replied, looking up to see the clouds inching toward them across the sky. "So much for that damn marine forecast."

Brad looked back to the dark wall against the eastern horizon and saw a flash. "Shit, Paul, that's lightning."

"Damn. Those bastards said east of Block Island. I don't mind some rain, but I'm not much interested in being out here in the middle of an electrical storm. Think we can beat it?"

"Sure. We're going a good six knots, right?"

"At least. Piece of cake."

"This sail has been too easy anyway," Brad grinned. "We could use a little bit of a challenge."

"Go below and grab the slickers, would you?" Soon, Paul and Brad were both wearing yellow rain jackets in preparation for the rain that now seemed inevitable.

The wind began to pick up and the seas began to rise. Before long, *The Wanderer* was slogging through two-foot swells that were growing and soon beginning to break over the bow. Paul could taste the saltwater from the spray. He felt the pull of the sails and estimated the wind at fifteen to twenty knots and getting stiffer.

"We need to lose some sail," he called out to Brad. "Let's reef the jib."

Brad pulled the reef line but nothing happened. "Something's wrong," he called back. "The line won't budge."

"See if it's caught on something."

"It's clear. It just won't pull."

The rain began to fall, lightly at first and then heavier. And then in torrents, pelting the men and their boat. The sky went dark and thunder sounded around them. The wind started blowing in gusts of twenty-five to thirty knots and, as the center of the storm crashed upon them, it began swirling from different directions.

Paul wiped the rain from his eyes and released the main sheet to allow the wind to spill from the sail but the line, just like the reef line, refused to move. *What the fuck?* Paul thought. "Get the main down!" he shouted to Brad.

Brad released the main halyard but the sail didn't fall. He crawled along the deck to the mast and pulled himself up and yanked on the luff of the sail but it was as if the sail was stuck in place. "It won't come down!" he yelled back to Paul.

"What do you mean?" Paul shouted.

"It must be caught on something!"

A streak of lightning crashed through the air with a loud crack. "Get away from the mast!" Paul shouted. Brad scrambled back to the cockpit.

The winds were now gale force and pushing *The Wanderer* over. She remained under full sail with the sails fixed tight as if by an inexplicable force, the wind continuing to push on them, driving the boat farther over on its side.

Paul spun the wheel to try to steer the boat into the wind, but the wheel was as frozen in place as the rigging. "Goddamn wheel won't turn!" he shouted to Brad. The boat was now on a forty-five-degree heel and both men hugged the high-side rail. Paul thought of the life jackets inside the cabin, now completely inaccessible from where they were positioned.

The wind howled and the rain was now blowing at them almost horizontally. The waves had risen to four feet and the boat pitched violently as the men hung on. It kept heeling over until Paul saw the mast touching the water. The boat was completely on its side now. Then a huge swell broke over the boat and the weight of the water on the sails drove the mast under. The cabin filled in an instant and before long there was just a small part of the hull above water, Paul and Brad tried to hold on but another swell rushed over them, knocking them both loose. Paul went under. He struggled back to the surface and looked to where *The Wanderer* was, but she was gone. He called out for his brother, but Brad was nowhere to be seen either. He shouted for him once more before another crushing wave broke over him, driving him under the raging water.

13

The worst part of Nicole's job was interviewing grieving people. And yet she knew that the interviews made for good reading. Everyone knew that the juiciest part of any story about a tragedy was the reaction of a loved one. People skimmed the rest of the article, looking for the inevitable quote from a spouse or parent.

And so it was that she found herself knocking on Doreen Dixon's door the morning after the bodies of her husband and brother-in-law had washed ashore not two miles from their home. It was three days after the accident. The Coast Guard had searched everywhere after Doreen had called and reported the boat overdue, but there had been so sign of boat nor men. Every inch of Half-Moon Island had been searched, too. Finally, a man fishing along the shoreline had spotted what he thought at first was debris from, perhaps, a passing cargo ship. But upon closer inspection, he could make out that the debris was, in actuality, a human body in a yellow rain slicker. By the time

Simon Barker arrived at the scene, a second body had been spotted about a hundred yards offshore. Identification was made and Barker had had the unenviable task of, once again, having to notify the next of kin.

Nicole knocked on the door again and soon Doreen herself answered. It was clear the woman hadn't slept in days. She wore no makeup, her hair needed brushing, her clothes were disheveled, and her eyes were red and lifeless.

"Yes?" she said.

"Mrs. Dixon? I'm Nicole Anders with the *New Liberty Gazette*. First of all, I want to say how sorry I am for your loss."

"Thank you."

"Of course everyone knows about your husband's tragic boating accident and the whole town is in shock. So I'm wondering if you might have anything you'd like us to say in the paper. We're going to print an update now that, well, now that, you know, they...found him and your brother-in-law. If there's anything you'd like to say about your husband that you'd like the community to know, this might be a good time. I'm sure you have something you'd like to share about him." There. Just like old Walt had taught her. The trick to getting a good quote is to make it all about the interviewee. Give them a reason to respond. Walt wasn't totally clueless. Nicole had to admit that in all his years of running a paper, he had learned a thing or two about effective journalism.

"Of course," said Doreen. "Please come in, Miss…I'm sorry what did you say your name was?"

"Anders. Nicole Anders."

"Please come in, Miss Anders."

Doreen clearly wasn't facing her grief alone. It was a quiet, somber household that Nicole stepped into, but far from an empty one. A woman with a baby, Brad's wife, Nicole surmised, was there, too. Maybe she wouldn't mind providing a quote. The kids were there, of course. An older couple that Nicole assumed to be Doreen's parents were also present. Everyone was sitting in the living room with the TV on very low, more or less as background noise. Other than that, the place was full of silence and vacant, empty stares. It was like a funeral. Maybe worse. Nicole could feel the melancholy, so thick that she had to resist the urge to turn and flee.

Doreen ushered Nicole into the kitchen where the two could talk privately. She offered Nicole a cup of coffee, but Nicole decided that she wanted to get her quote and get out.

"What would you like to know about Paul?" Doreen asked.

"Well, you know, something that might be of interest to the community. Like…well, maybe you could tell me what kind of a man he was."

"Oh, he was a wonderful man," Doreen said. And then she rambled on about how they met in college, and about their wedding, their kids, their lives together. Nicole had to steady herself, forcing a smile through the gloom she could feel was enveloping her.

Doreen said that she couldn't believe that Paul and Brad were gone. "It's like a nightmare," she said. "You just hope you'll wake up." In that instant, Nicole was hit by a very distinct, unmistakable feeling that made her shudder. It was a strange perception of something dark and horrid, a sense, perhaps, of death itself. Doreen didn't notice the shudder, continuing on about the upcoming service to be held at New Liberty First Presbyterian Church. Finally, Nicole talked about Paul's relationship with Brad, how close the brothers were.

"Would you like to see some pictures of the two of them together?"

"Oh, that's quite all right," Nicole said, the misery of the house continuing to press down upon her. "I think I've bothered you enough. I should probably be going now."

"Come on down to the basement with me. Paul had some great family pictures. Really, it'll only take a second."

"Well, I really need to be getting back to the office..."

"Please?"

Doreen's eyes were welling up and Nicole realized through the gloom that this woman needed someone at that very moment to share her thoughts with, regardless of how distressing Nicole found the home to be. "Okay, sure," she said.

Doreen led Nicole down the basement steps. With each step downward it seemed to Nicole that the grim atmosphere of the house was becoming heavier and heavier. She found herself having trouble breathing. Tears formed in her eyes. *My God, it's just like the Horton house*, she thought to herself. By the time they reached the bottom step, Nicole felt overwhelmed by the grief, as if she were in the throes of a deep, bottomless sorrow.

"The pictures are on his desk," Nicole heard Doreen say through the fog of despair that had clutched her. "He took them down to put that damn picture up. Oh, and look, it's crooked again."

Nicole managed to raise her head and when she did, she saw the crooked painting of the sailboats.

Doreen continued. "Well, anyway, take a look at this picture of him and Brad. See how happy they were?"

She turned to hand Nicole the small, framed picture, but caught only a glimpse of Nicole fleeing up the stairs.

"I'm so sorry!" Nicole called down on her way out. "I'm afraid I'm not feeling well!"

A moment later Doreen heard the front door opening and then slamming shut.

———◆———

Nicole drove for twenty minutes. No direction in particular. The important thing was to drive. Away from the Dixon house. At last, she found herself back in town and felt calmed by the energy of the people walking about. The feelings of death and doom seemed to dissipate. She had just a sense of those feelings now, the way you have a sense of gloom after awakening from a nightmare, the sense mitigated by an even stronger sense of relief.

She pulled into a parking space on Main Street a block from the *Gazette* offices. She had to make the phone call, but damned if she was going to make it in front of Walt. Like he'd understand.

She scrolled through the notes on her tablet until she came to the phone number and dialed. *Please be Jill and not Randy*, she thought. Jill had been nice. Jill had invited her in. It was Randy who had sent her on her way.

"Hello?"

Jill. Phew.

"Hi, Jill? I don't know if you remember me, but I'm Nicole Anders with the *New Liberty Gazette*." Nicole tried her best to put a smile into her voice.

"Oh, yes, hello. I remember. You were writing an article on mental illness. I'm sorry, but I really don't have anything to say. You know, we sold the house. We spend all of our time here in Cape May now."

"Yes, I saw where the house was sold. That's partly why I'm calling. I know it's going to sound weird, but I have a question about some of the items I saw that day when I was in your living room, and where those items might be now. Personal questions. Nothing for the paper, I assure you."

"Some of the items?"

"Well, yes, for example, do you remember those gargoyle bookends?"

Jill chuckled. "Oh, yes, those hideous things. How could I forget?"

"And the painting of the sailboats."

"Yes, I remember. What about it?"

Yes, what about it? Nicole wondered the same thing. What about the painting? What about the bookends? How could she explain it to Jill? Did Jill even know the bookends were used in a brutal murder? What would she say if she knew that the painting was hanging crooked that very moment over the desk of the victim of a fatal sailboat accident? How could

Nicole explain her interest in bookends and paintings without sounding like a complete crackpot?

Finally, she said, "Well, the thing is, I have a friend who's moving into a new home and she has rather unique taste in décor. She's kind of the artsy type, you know? Anyway, I'm racking my brains to try to think of something out of the ordinary for a house-warming gift and I just remembered the interesting things in your living room. I remember seeing a unique birdcage there, too. I mean, I hate to bother you, but I'm kind of desperate. I'm afraid a house-plant or blender just isn't going to cut it with this particular friend, you know what I mean?" There. That sounded plausible.

"Sure, I understand."

"So when you sold the house, what did you do with its contents?"

"Well, a lot of stuff went to Goodwill and the Salvation Army. You know, the furniture and clothes and such. Randy kept some of his dad's tools and I kept some miscellaneous items. But things like what you're talking about we took to a consignment shop."

"A consignment shop?"

"Yes, in fact, it was the same shop where my mother-in-law had bought them in the first place. It's the one on Garner Street."

Three blocks over. Next to the ice cream store.

"Yes, I know it," Nicole said. "Well, thank you, Jill. That's very helpful. I'll pop my head in there. I'm sure there might be something of interest to my friend."

"You're welcome. Good luck!"

Nicole hung up and opened her tablet again. She scrolled through it, perusing some of the notes she'd jotted down over the last few months. Then she got out of her car and decided to walk the three blocks to the consignment shop. It was a perfectly lovely day for a stroll downtown. Passing the storefronts, it became easy to forget the gloom and melancholy of the morning. Maybe all of this was just in her head. What was she expecting to find in the consignment shop, anyway? Some things are probably best left alone. Maybe she should just get some ice cream and call it a day.

Nevertheless, something compelled Nicole to enter the little store. And something further compelled her to ask the girl behind the counter about the items from the Horton house. Finally, she had to ask about one more item. There it was in her notes, staring out at her. Maybe the strangest item of all, and the one that could possibly confirm the impossible: a pair of flameless candles.

"Yes," the girl said. "We had a set of those here. Someone bought them a month or so ago. She mentioned that she planned on giving them as a housewarming gift at a dinner party that night, as I recall. Why do you ask?"

"No reason," said Nicole. "Just...curious."

And then Nicole left the shop and walked back out into the sunshine of the street, the warmth providing scant defense against the cold shiver that was running down her spine.

14

"**D**emonic *what*?"

"Demonic infestation," Nicole repeated. "Walt, it's a real thing. I mean, the Catholic Church believes it. Why do you think they have exorcisms?"

"I thought exorcisms were for possessed people, not things."

"They can be for either."

Walt had better things to do than listen to Nicole ramble on about some crazy occult gibberish, but obviously she wasn't going to leave him alone until he heard her out. She'd come in that morning bleary-eyed, talking about how she'd been up all night scouring the internet. Then, pacing around the office, she'd launched into this cockamamie theory of hers. Walt sat back in his chair resigned to the fact that he had no choice but to listen.

"Experts agree that objects can be cursed," Nicole continued. "Sometimes unintentionally, like a knife used in a murder, for example. It can become cursed by the circumstances. This allows demonic forces to possess it. It's called 'exercising dominion.'"

"Experts. What experts?"

"Experts, Walt. There's a whole community of people who study this stuff. Scientifically."

"Oh, really?"

"Yes, and I'll be interviewing a few of them for the piece."

"What piece, Nicole?"

"The piece I'm going to put together on the demonic infestation of the items associated with the deaths of the Hortons, Lisa and Ethan Rhodes, the three co-eds, and Paul Dixon and his brother."

There it was. Walt knew she was building up to something. "Look, Nicole—"

"Walt, all this time you've refused to believe there was a connection. But there is! Every one of these people owned, at some point, an item from the consignment shop on Garner Street. And, as it turns out, from the same booth. Some of them owned the same item. The Hortons had them all. The Rhodes owned the flameless candles. The co-eds had the bookends. Paul Dixon owned the old oil painting."

"And you know what science would call all that? Coincidence, Nicole."

"Walt, two days ago I wouldn't have believed it either. I'm just as skeptical as you are about this kind of stuff. But there's no denying the chain of custody of the items in question. And according to my research—"

Walt rolled his eyes, but Nicole pushed ahead.

"According to my research, the demonic possession of objects is not that uncommon. I don't mean that it happens all the time, but there have been many documented cases of evil forces exercising dominion over objects."

"Yeah? Name one."

Nicole picked up her tablet. "Pittsburgh, 1997: a woman was murdered by her boyfriend who hit her on the head repeatedly with a brick. You know where the brick came from? It was originally part of a brick wall that surrounded a nineteenth century graveyard for the criminally insane. Edmonton, 2011: a farmer ran his wife through with a pitchfork, a pitchfork, Walt, that he'd picked up at a yard sale of a house where a double murder had taken place. In both cases, by the way, friends and family were shocked by the killings. Nobody believed the guy from Pittsburgh or the farmer from Edmonton would have been capable of doing what they did. Sound familiar?"

Walt remained silent.

"Have you ever heard of the Aokigahara Forest in Japan?"

Walt shook his head.

"It's called the 'Suicide Forest.' Since 1960, more than a hundred people have hiked into the forest and killed themselves. Now it's become something of a trendy spot for suicides, kind of like the Golden Gate Bridge. But, Walt, there are many cases of people going in there without any inclination of offing themselves, but then that's exactly what they ended up doing. Throwing themselves off cliffs and so forth. Some hang themselves. It's an entire *forest* that's demonically possessed."

"A haunted forest, Nicole?"

"No, not haunted. Much worse than haunted. Haunted means there are spirits about. They might even be good spirits. Ghosts. People who have died but maybe don't know it. They're lingering around, unable or unwilling to move on, stuck between this life and, well, whatever comes next. What I'm talking about are things, even whole places, like houses or forests, that come under the control—the *dominion*—of evil forces."

"I don't know, Nicole..."

"You see, it's like this: an object becomes cursed by its circumstances—a gruesome murder, most typically. The object doesn't become evil, per se, but it opens itself up for demonic possession. It's cursed by the evil that was present, as though it's poisoned by it. And so it seeks, in some way, the source of the curse, like a child seeking its mother. *Res clamat ad dominum.* 'An object calls for its owner.' What happens is that the item in question becomes what's called a 'conduit of malediction.' It becomes a portal, in other words. A portal that allows evil to enter. Walt, you can choose not to believe, but I'm here to tell you that I *felt* that evil. I felt it in the Horton's house. It's in the Dixon's house, too, and it's a hundred times more prevalent in their basement where that goddamn painting is hanging. If you went there, you'd feel the same thing. I thought I was going to suffocate down in that basement. I felt like my life was in danger, or at least my sanity."

"Nicole, listen to yourself. All this talk about demonic stuff—"

"Do you believe in God, Walt?"

"Sure, I guess so."

"A good God?"

"Of course."

"Well, Walt, if good exists, then so does evil. It's basic philosophy. Everything exists relative to something else. Once something comes into the universe, its opposite enters, too. What would it mean for something to be good if there were no evil by which to measure goodness? Can you conceive of light without thinking of darkness? What's the concept of hot without the concept of cold?"

Walt furrowed his brow, his mind trying to catch up to Nicole's discourse. "Well, I—"

"C.S. Lewis said, 'There is no neutral ground in the universe. Every square inch, every split second is claimed by God and counterclaimed by Satan.' Now, truthfully, I don't know what to think about God and Satan. I've never been exactly what you'd call religious. I went to Sunday school when I was little, but I couldn't tell you the last time I stepped into a church. But it's hard to deny that there's something to the whole good/evil dichotomy. And I think we've been seeing it play out right before our eyes. Walt, if that's not newsworthy, then what the hell is?"

Nicole had done her homework, that was for sure. And her ideas were not, in and of themselves, uninteresting. But this was the *Gazette*. Nicole's ideas were not appropriate and that was that. "Nicole," Walt declared, "we're not running a metaphysics periodical. Why can't you understand that we're running a small-town newspaper? You have to think of the *readership*."

"I am, Walt. Come on, you've heard it. All the talk in the town about the tragedies? Everywhere you go! Nobody is talking about anything else. Our 'readership,' in case you haven't noticed, is obsessed with the killings. You don't think they'd be interested in a piece that offers an explanation?"

"You mean a theory."

"Okay, then, a theory."

In truth, Walt had to confess that Nicole was definitely right about one thing. People *were* talking. Is it possible he was missing an opportunity? Hell, maybe a piece on the connection, if there really was one, between all the killings would sell some papers. Walt wasn't blind to the numbers. He'd printed out the latest year-to-date income statement himself just two days before and it wasn't pretty. But such an article could not be done in a shlocky way. This wasn't a gossip rag; it was the venerable *New Liberty Gazette*. Regardless of the numbers, Walt was carrying on a proud tradition that went back to his grandfather.

He was silent for a long moment, arms crossed, looking up at the ceiling, thinking. Nicole knew instinctively not to say anything. She was about to make the sale and she didn't want to blow it now.

Finally, Walt spoke. "Let's say I agreed that a piece on this connection of yours might be interesting."

Nicole started to smile.

"Now, I'm not saying I'm agreeing, Nicole. I mean hypothetically."

"Of course," Nicole nodded, dropping the smile.

"It would have to be done right. You talked about interviewing people. People with scientific backgrounds. They'd have to be credible."

"Naturally."

"With bona fide credentials."

"Of course."

"So who do you have lined up?"

"Glad you asked. I'm going to see one this afternoon, as a matter of fact. I have to meet with someone beforehand and then I'm going. You want to come along? Then you can see for yourself."

"Yes, I do, Nicole. Because I'm telling you, if we're going to do this, we're going to do it right. Okay? No cutting corners, no sloppy reporting, no printing of rumors or innuendo. Facts, Nicole. Hard, cold facts. Understood?"

"Understood," Nicole replied, and now she allowed herself to smile.

⸻ ⬥ ⸻

The person Nicole had to meet before her appointment with the expert was Donnie Olson of the New Liberty Fire Department. She had called him the night before and explained what she was doing. They'd agreed to meet in the parking lot of a local coffee shop. Donnie was already there when Nicole pulled up. She parked her Jeep beside his truck. Donnie got out of the truck and slid into Nicole's passenger seat with a brown paper bag.

"Is that them?" Nicole asked.

"Sure is," Donnie replied, handing over the bag.

Nicole opened it and peaked inside. "God, you were right, Donnie, they look brand new. How can that be possible? Listen, I can't thank you enough for bringing these. I know how much trouble you could get in for taking them from the station."

"I don't care, Nicole. I don't mind telling you that this whole thing has been freaking me out. And to answer your question, it's *not* possible. It's utterly impossible, as a matter of fact. It makes zero sense. I'm really glad you're looking into it. So who is this woman you're going to see again?"

"A parapsychologist. You know, a psychic. She's trained in these sorts of things. Deals with them all the time."

"So you think it's...what? Some kind of supernatural thing?"

"I wouldn't say supernatural. I've been doing a lot of research. Turns out there are a shitload of things we just don't understand, but that doesn't mean they're not part of the natural world. You know, there was a time when people didn't understand thunderstorms and believed they were conjured up by the gods. They would have called them supernatural, but eventually science figured thunderstorms out. Donnie, I'm beginning to think there might be whole dimensions we just don't yet understand, but dimensions that are a part of this world as much as you and me."

"Well, if you ask me, this thing comes from some evil part of the world. And you think the fire is connected with the other stuff?"

"That's the theory. That's what I'm looking to find out and I think this parapsychologist can help. Listen, I better get back to the office, Donnie. I'll get these back to you tomorrow, I promise. Thanks again."

"Sure, Nicole. I'll be looking forward to hearing how it went." Donnie got out of the Jeep and then turned back to Nicole once more. "Hey," he said, "you be careful, okay? I got a feeling that this is some dangerous shit you're getting involved with, Nicole. Really dangerous."

Nicole smiled. "Thanks, Donnie. I'll be careful, don't worry.

15

"So what's in the bag?"

"Open it."

Walt was in the passenger seat of Nicole's Jeep not entirely sure of where they were going or why. He opened the bag and took a look inside.

"Candles?" he said.

"Flameless candles," Nicole added.

"So?"

"Walt, they're not just any flameless candles. They're *the* flameless candles."

"What do you mean *the* flameless can—Oh, Nicole, you can't be serious. The ones from the fire?"

"Yep."

"How did you get them?"

"I have a source at the fire department and I—"

"Don't tell me anymore, I don't want to know."

Walt pulled one of the candles out of the bag and held it in his hand, turning it around and inspecting it closely. "It looks...it looks...*new.*"

"Right? That's what I've been talking about. Walt, do you know what the average temperature of a house fire is?"

"No clue."

"Eleven-hundred degrees Fahrenheit. Eleven. Hundred. Degrees."

Walt was quiet. Finally he put the candle back in the bag and said, "So where are we taking them?"

"To someone who can help us test the concept of demonic infestation."

"And who's that?"

"Her name is Olive Ramsey. She lives in Stonington and she's a psychic."

"A psychic? I don't know, Nicole. Remember what I said about credible sources..."

"Believe me, Dr. Ramsey is credible."

"*Doctor* Ramsey? What is she a doctor of?"

"Parapsychology, as a matter of fact."

Walt sighed.

"It's a real science, Walt. She has a genuine PhD in it. There are people in the world who have natural psychic abilities, people who are telepathic or clairvoyant. She's one of those people and she's made a career out of studying the paranormal."

"But, Nicole—"

"Do you remember the case of Jessica Maxwell?"

"Sounds vaguely familiar."

"Jessica Maxwell was the eight-year-old girl from Hartford who went missing about five years ago. The case went on for months. The police searched everywhere and followed every lead. The whole town was on the lookout. Posters were put up all over Connecticut."

"And they finally found her body in the woods, as I recall. About thirty miles outside of town."

"Right. And they even made an arrest eventually. Some loner who was convicted and sentenced to life."

"So?"

"So you know who led them to the body? That's right, Walt. Olive Ramsey."

"Seriously?"

"Seriously. She found the little girl's body when nobody else could. You can look it up. And a case like that is not so unusual. Police departments have been using psychics for missing persons cases for years."

Walt sensed Nicole's sincerity. Whatever he believed, he had to respect that about her. And the condition of the candle was stupefying. How to explain it? "So tell me what you expect from this doctor," he said.

"Well, I'm hoping she can get a sense of the mood or state of these candles. To see whether some...thing, or some force, is exercising dominion over them. To see if they're somehow possessed."

"Okay, Nicole, but I have one condition."

"Sure."

"You can*not* lead her on. She can know nothing of where the candles came from. Not a word. Not a hint. Let's just put them in front of her and see what she says."

"Of course. I would never interview anybody in a leading way. I'm a professional journalist, you know. Or maybe you haven't noticed."

"Okay, okay," Walt said. "Sorry. Just making sure." And then he reached back into the bag and took a candle out again, holding it, and looking at it long and hard.

———— ❧ ————

Dr. Olive Ramsey was in her seventies with round glasses and gray hair that she wore long. Her house was a modest bungalow on a quiet, tree-lined street. Nicole and Walt sat across from her at a table in her parlor, a busy, colorful room with antique furniture and walls filled with little shelves of knick-knacks, photos, framed letters presumably from satisfied clients, and one framed, yellowed newspaper page with a headline that read, "Psychic Leads Cops to Murder Victim."

After the usual pleasantries, she thanked Nicole for calling for an appointment and asked what she could help with. Nicole took the candles out and placed them on the table in front of her.

"We're curious about these," Nicole said.

"I see," said Dr. Ramsey.

"Is there anything you can tell us about them?"

"I can try. Do they have some kind of meaning to you?"

"Maybe," Walt interjected. "But maybe not. We're hoping *you* can tell *us*."

"Of course," Dr. Ramsey smiled, sensing the skepticism. "Often times, objects do have a distinct sense about them."

"Either good or evil, right?" Nicole said. Walt shot her a sideways glance as a reminder of their agreement not to lead Dr. Ramsey on.

"For the most part," Dr. Ramsey replied, "but it's not often that convenient a dichotomy. It's more of a spectrum, you see. Most objects are neutral. But over time, through ownership, they can become tainted. They can begin to lean one way or the other and to varying degrees. The type of ownership sets the general course. It's called holding dominion over the article."

Now it was Nicole's turn to shoot a sideways glance at Walt, as if to say *told you so*.

"It has always been thus," Dr. Ramsey continued. "Thousands of years ago, ancient religions held certain objects in high or low esteem, not necessarily because of the type of object, but because of what was sensed about it. Ancient shamans would decipher the meaning or significance of an object and determine whether it was a portend of fortune or misfortune. Rituals were practiced to either bless the object or to rid it of evil spirits. There is much history to the idea of dominion, going all the way back to Mesopotamia, and it remains an integral part of theology today. The Catholic practice of exorcism, for example, is based entirely on the idea. More commonly, you see instances of priests blessing all sorts of things, like a house someone just moves into, for example, as a way to confer positive dominion over the residence."

Nicole nodded along as Dr. Ramsey spoke. Walt sat more or less impassively, but seemed, to Nicole, to be a little less skeptical than when they'd entered the parlor. Dr. Ramsey was certainly knowledgeable. Walt had to admit that, Nicole thought. And she spoke with authority. She spoke with experience.

"Well, then," Dr. Ramsey said, "let me get a good look at what you've brought me here today." She put on her reading glasses and leaned in toward the candles, scrutinizing them. Several minutes went by, the only sound in the room the rhythmic pendulum swing of a grandfather clock in the corner.

Finally, Dr. Ramsey leaned back in her chair and took a deep breath, then closed her eyes for several seconds. She opened her eyes and gazed at the ceiling for a few more moments before saying, "I'm sorry. I seem to be blocked."

Walt and Nicole glanced at each other. "What does that mean exactly?" Walt said.

"Well, you see, I can't get any reading on them. It happens sometimes. It might be that there's nothing significant about the candles at all. Nothing that comes forth, anyway. Nothing positive, nothing negative. Again, I'm sorry. I sense you were expecting another reaction?"

Walt looked over at Nicole, who looked positively dejected, and said, "We weren't really expecting anything, were we, Nicole?"

Nicole was about to answer when Dr. Ramsey reached for one of the candles, wrapping her hand around it. Immediately, she let it go, startling both Nicole and Walt with a chilling, high-pitched scream. *"Ahhh!"* she cried grabbing her hand in obvious pain. *"Oh God, it's on fire!"* she wailed.

Nicole and Walt sat stunned, both of them staring at Dr. Ramsey in disbelief, seeing blisters forming on her hand where it had been seared by the heat of the cold, flameless, perfect candle.

"Walt, I can understand this coming from Nicole—no offense, Nicole—but from you?" Simon Barker leaned forward in his chair, looking at Walt, eyebrows raised.

Walt and Nicole sat across from the detective at his desk, having explained to him the incident in Dr. Ramsey's parlor. The candles were sitting harmlessly between them. Twenty minutes earlier, Dr. Ramsey had gathered herself together and issued a warning to Walt and Nicole. "There is a rare form of evil in these candles," she had said. "Please be careful. It is not safe. It is a dangerous, malignant conduit."

"Well...what should we do with them?" Nicole asked.

"Good can never regain possession of them. They need to be destroyed. Broken, burned, and buried. I wish the both of you peace and light, but I must ask that you take these candles away now. Please, do be careful. Above all else, do *not* bring the candles into your own home. Bringing evil into one's home is as bringing evil into one's heart." Then, nursing her hand, she strode to the front door and opened it for them.

Nicole touched the candles, feeling nothing at all, and quickly slid them back into the bag and she and

Walt left Dr. Ramsey's house. She was unnerved, but not as much as Walt seemed to be. She glanced over at him in the car. He was pale, his eyes wide. Nicole had never seen him like that.

For Walt's part, he was clearly shaken. He still didn't know exactly what to believe, but perhaps what was most disturbing was that he no longer knew what *not* to believe. Both agreed that Detective Barker needed to be made aware of what they'd just experienced and they set off for his office. Nicole set the candles in the backseat for the trip to Barker's office, but Walt couldn't stop himself from glancing back at them every thirty seconds or so to make sure they hadn't burst into flames.

"We'll be fine," Nicole said. "Dr. Ramsey is a channel. She can experience things we can't. Sitting there in that bag, those candles are harmless." Nicole spoke calmly and Walt knew that she was much less shaken than he was, almost as if she'd expected something like this. He didn't like that position—the boss, the man, being so much more spooked than his young subordinate. He tried to keep it together, tried to convey a low-key demeanor but there was no hiding the fact that he was rattled to the core.

And now, in Barker's office, he had to explain the inexplicable and the task was not going well.

Barker picked up one of the candles and turned it around in his hand. "I'm not feeling a thing," he said. "By the way, does the FD know you took these?"

"All I can say, Simon, is that you should have been there," Walt offered. "Tell him, Nicole. Tell him about demonic infestation and the concept of dominion."

"It happens," Nicole said. "Ownership by good or evil is a real thing, detective. Look, believe me, we know this sounds far-fetched, but if you start connecting the dots between all of the items that were, in some way, associated with this summer's tragedies, well, it's beyond coincidence. Something is going on."

"The consignment shop, Simon," Walt added. "Nicole has traced all of this to a consignment shop on Garner Street. That place next to the ice cream shop?"

"Sure, I know it. But what am I supposed to do, Walt? Arrest the proprietor for selling items possessed by the devil? Christ, guys, maybe we should just start burning witches while we're at it."

"You could question them," Nicole suggested.

"Nicole, I have no interest in becoming a laughingstock in this town. I'm a detective. I deal in facts. People trust me to do so. I'm not about to go around questioning people without sufficient cause."

"But—"

"Rational, *reasonable* cause. Not because someone somewhere suspects that the devil has possessed some items for sale in a downtown shop."

"We didn't say—"

"Now, look, both of you, I don't doubt that you thought you saw something out of the ordinary, maybe even something disturbing. Hey, weird shit happens. I'm not going to deny that. But I'm sure that in the light of reason, you'll come to see that at least some of this might have just been in your imagination. Now, doesn't that sound reasonable?"

"Bullshit!" Nicole said, rising out of her chair. "You weren't there!"

"Nicole, we see what we want to see. That's all I'm saying."

"Come on, Walt. We don't need this crap." Nicole reached toward the desk, snatched the candle, turned, and strode out of Barker's office.

Walt stood up slowly and turned to follow her. Then he stopped and glanced back at Barker. "How long have you known me, Simon?" he said quietly.

"A long time, Walt. A damn long time."

"Ever know me to let my imagination run away with anything?"

"Can't say that I have, Walt."

"I didn't think so." Having made his point, Walt walked out of Barker's office to catch up with Nicole out in the street.

Barker leaned back in his chair and thought about what a strange meeting he'd just had. Inanimate objects as conduits of evil? What had Nicole called it? Demonic infestation? Dominion? Amazing what some people will believe, he thought. And now Walt believed her, that was the really surprising part. Old Walt.

Of course the idea was ludicrous. Wasn't it? But how to explain the burns on the psychic's hands? That was strange, no doubt about it. Some kind of trick? But she'd had no idea the candles were involved in a fire. And why *were* the candles in such good condition?

And then Barker thought about those damn gargoyle bookends and the improbability of a sober, smart, rational college coed going nuts in the middle of the night and bashing in the brains of not one, but two close friends as they slept.

Nonetheless, logic and reason ruled the world. What was the use in inventing preposterous theories for simple coincidences? The simplest explanation is always the best, Barker thought to himself. We see what we want to see. And then, feeling suddenly alone and trying to ward off the shiver that had been threatening to seize him for the last half-hour, he left his office to go to the breakroom. A cup of coffee wouldn't hurt and maybe someone would be there to talk to. About anything. Anything other than candles and bookends and demonic infestation.

16

Nicole didn't sleep all night. She tossed and turned thinking about the day's happenings. She'd gone home that evening after dropping the candles off with Donnie at the firehouse, had the better part of a bottle of wine, taken a long, hot bath, and then slid into bed. Only sleep never came. She wondered if Walt had slept at all. Donnie probably didn't. His eyes had gotten huge when Nicole had told him all about the trip to Dr. Ramsey's. After that, he was scared to even touch the candles. Nicole had assured him they were safe in the firehouse where they had been, but warned him not to take them home. "You don't have to worry about that!" Donnie had said.

What had mostly gone through Nicole's mind as she tossed and turned that night was what to do next. Now that she knew about the items from the consignment shop, what should she do with that information? Naturally, she was still thinking about the piece that she was going to write for the *Gazette*. The *Gazette*? Hell, this was the kind of article that could end up in the *New York Times*. She had to admit that the idea gave her a little thrill of excitement. But then she thought of the tragedies that had created the story in the first place and the thrill morphed into a small feeling of guilt. But, hey, war correspondents don't feel guilty when they do a great job of reporting from the front lines, right? It's their job and they should take pride in it. That thought made her feel better.

Still, it raised another concern. What was her *obligation*, given what she now knew? Of course her obligation as a journalist was clear. To report what she had uncovered about the nature of the objects from the consignment shop, backed up with the facts at hand. But what about her obligation as a human being? As a member of the community? How many more items from the consignment shop were out there? People needed to know the dangers. If a food distributor discovered that they had been selling tainted meat, wouldn't they be obligated to immediately recall the meat? She'd already made up her mind to retrieve the candle from the firehouse and destroy it as Dr. Ramsey had advised. But the consignment shop needed to know what they had on hand. Somewhere around 4 a.m., she'd decided she was going to pay the shop another visit, this time to talk to the owner. She had planned on going anyway at some point. If Barker wasn't going to question the proprietor, then she would. But now there was a greater sense of urgency about it.

At 9 a.m., the shop opened. Nicole walked in at 9:01. Debra Jennings had owned the shop for the past dozen years and as Nicole entered, Debra was straightening out some items on a shelf. Upon the tinkle of the bell above the door, she turned around. "Hi. Can I help you?"

"Maybe," Nicole said. "Are you the owner?"

"Yes. I'm Debra."

"Hi, Debra, I'm Nicole Anders with the *Gazette*."

"Pleased to meet you. What can I do for you?"

At 4 a.m., in the dark of her bedroom, without sleep, after the strange and disturbing visit to a psychic, the idea of spilling what she'd learned to Debra Jennings seemed entirely appropriate to Nicole. "You have to stop selling everything in your shop until we can somehow separate the evil items from the good items!" she imagined herself saying. Now, in the cold light of day, she realized how ridiculous that was going to sound.

Nicole stood silently for a long moment, fumbling in her mind for just the right words to convey the purpose of her visit.

"Miss?" Debra said. "Are you okay? Is there something I can help you with?"

"Oh, I'm fine," Nicole said at last, managing a smile, "I was just wondering, well, I mean...do you remember a set of gargoyle bookends that you had for sale here earlier this summer?"

"Oh, I sure do," Debra chuckled. "Very unique. I'm sorry, were you interested in them? They sold quite some time ago."

"No, I was just curious. How about an old oil painting of two sailboats racing each other?"

"Yes, I seem to remember that, too."

"Or a pair of flameless candles?"

"Yes. Why do you ask? I'm sorry, did you say you were with the *Gazette*? Nicole, was it? Nicole, what's your interest in all of these items?"

"Listen, Debra, I know this is going to sound strange, but they all have something in common."

"Yes, I know."

"They all—wait, you do?"

"Sure. They all came from the same house."

"They did?"

"Yes. What did *you* think they all had in common?"

"Whose house?"

"Well, her name is Elaine, but that's about all I can say. I'm really not at liberty to pass along the personal information of the consignors, you know. Can you please tell me why you're asking about this stuff?"

Nicole weighed in her mind how much to tell Debra. She probably wouldn't believe it anyway. Finally, she decided to leave out the supernatural parts and stick with the more earth-bound facts. "The truth,

Debra, is that I'm doing a story on the summer tragedies New Liberty has endured."

Debra nodded somberly. "I see."

"Yes, and one thing I can share with you is that all of these items were, at one point, in the homes of the people who died."

"Really?"

"Yes, strange as it might seem."

"Wow. I had no idea. That sure is a wacky coincidence."

Not really, Nicole wanted to say. It's not a coincidence at all. It's demonic infestation. Evil forces are exercising their dominion. Instead, she said, "Yes, isn't it? So, anyway, I was wondering if you could tell me anything about where the items came from. You said the owner's name is Elaine?"

"Well, yes, but, again, I can't give away any personal information."

"Can you tell me if there was anything...strange about her? Anything out of the ordinary?"

"No, just an average woman." Then Debra was thoughtful for a moment and lowered her voice. "I'll tell you this, though. People keep returning her items. Except for the ones you mentioned, plus a couple of others, like a throw rug, any time someone buys something out of booth 15, it gets returned."

"Seriously?"

"In fact, I was planning on calling Elaine to tell her that we cannot continue to stock her items. We make some exceptions for returns and exchanges, but it's been pretty ridiculous with her stuff."

"When were you going to call her."

"I don't know. Probably today some time."

"Can you do me a favor?"

"If I can."

"Here's my card. Can you call me when Elaine comes in to pick everything up?"

"Hmm...I don't know..."

"I'll just swing by like a customer. My office is just three blocks from here. I swear, I won't let on that you called me. I'll just engage her in some light conversation, that's all."

"I really shouldn't. But I have to admit, I am curious. I've never had to call someone to tell them we were going to stop selling their stuff before. And this idea that the items were somehow connected to the deaths..."

"Right? Isn't it fascinating?"

"Okay," Debra said, taking Nicole's card. "When she comes in to take everything out, I'll let you know."

"Thanks, Debra. I really appreciate it." Nicole smiled, shook Debra's hand, and left the shop. Then she walked toward the office, wondering what in the world she was going to ask this Elaine woman when she saw her.

Nicole sat at her desk considering the to-do list before her. There was the recent rash of small burglaries that she had to write an article about. Walt wanted a short profile piece on a recent high school grad who'd been accepted to West Point. A town meeting was scheduled for the next week about refurbishing the municipal marina and Nicole knew she had to interview someone for that, too.

She couldn't bring herself to start on any of it. She took another sip of her coffee and then pulled out her phone and decided to call Dr. Olive Ramsey instead. There was something she needed to know.

Dr. Ramsey answered on the first ring.

"I'm really sorry to bother you, Dr. Ramsey," Nicole began, "but, well, first of all, how's your hand?"

"It's fine, Nicole," Dr. Ramsey said. "And you're not bothering me at all. I'm glad you called. Frankly, the blisters were gone within minutes of your leaving here with the candles."

"What? You can't be serious. I saw your hand. It looked like you had third degree burns!"

"Exactly. Don't you see, Nicole? That only serves to further illuminate just how sinister the forces are that are holding dominion over those candles."

"How so?"

"It's a taunt, Nicole. It's the evil essentially showing off, letting us know it carries the power of life or death. It can burn; it can heal. That means that whatever has infested the candles is free to choose."

"I'm afraid I don't understand, Dr. Ramsey."

"If something is evil by nature, it can't help but be evil. That's its nature. Right? But if something freely *chooses* to be evil or to exercise evil, that means it's operating with malice and intent. It's intelligent, Nicole. It's not just evil; it's *creatively* evil. It's intelligently evil. And that makes it infinitely more dangerous. Do you see?"

"I think so..."

"Nicole, I have seen minor examples of this sort of thing before. Objects that deliver bad luck or maybe bring sadness into a home. But this...this is over the top evil that we're talking about. You have to understand what we're dealing with here. Now please tell me you did what I told you to do with the candles."

"Well, that's why I'm calling, actually. They're back where they were before—the New Liberty Fire Department. I had sort of borrowed them. Kind of illegally. To be perfectly honest with you, they're being held as evidence in a mysterious fire."

"Yes, I assumed something like that. People died in that fire, didn't they?"

"Yes. Yes, two people were killed. But, Dr. Ramsey, I need to know more about this idea of destroying the candles. I mean in general terms. The idea of destroying something that is demonically infested. How does that work exactly?"

"When a force holds dominion over an object, it holds it over the object in the form the object has taken. The candles, for instance, are being held as candles. If they cease to be candles, if they're broken apart, in other words, the force loses its control."

"But you said something about burning them and burying them."

"Yes, it's called 'specter dispersal.' It's just a theory, which I happen to subscribe to. It's like an insurance policy. Even though an item may be destroyed, there might still be the specter of evil lurking about what's left of it. Energy is neither created nor destroyed, after all. Threads of whatever held dominion over the article can still be present. And so it's best to change the molecular configuration of it. Transforming it into flame is the most efficient means of doing this. Then, the melted result should be divided up and buried in at least two different locations."

"I see."

Dr. Ramsey was quiet for a moment and then said, "Nicole, you have to get those candles."

"But I—"

"By any means necessary. Do you understand?"

"Of course."

"Then break them apart and bring the pieces to me."

"Really? Are you sure? I mean, after yesterday..."

"I'm sure. We can't take any chances, Nicole. I will perform the dispersal ritual. There's an incantation that goes with it. I haven't performed it for a long time but I remember it well. We'll burn the pieces, divide the melted remains, and bury them. It's the only way."

"Okay. I'll get them from the fire department again and be in touch."

"Nicole, I don't mean to frighten you, but you have to understand that whatever is acting upon those candles is fully aware of your presence now. Please be careful. I hope to hear from you very soon."

"I understand. And you will. Thank you again, Dr. Ramsey."

Nicole hung up and involuntarily shuddered. She sat for a while contemplating the words of explanation and warning she'd just received. *Be brave, Nicole,* she told herself. *Like Mom always taught you, take the word 'scared' out of your vocabulary.* But right now, that was more easily said than done.

Nicole opened her laptop and began tapping away. She had all the pieces for the story now except for the origin of the objects, but she knew that Debra

Jennings would be calling as soon as the owner of the objects came into the shop. In the meantime, she figured she'd start with the murder-suicide of the Hortons. She'd end with the specter dispersal theory and her eye-witnessing of the ritual as performed by Dr. Ramsey, sort of offering a solution to the problems the town had faced. Everything in between would practically write itself.

"Nicole, what are you working on?"

Nicole looked up to see that Walt had emerged from his office.

"What do you think?" she said, and then she resumed her typing.

"Well stop it," Walt said.

"Huh?"

Walt pulled a chair up to Nicole's desk and spoke quietly. "Nicole, I've been up all night thinking about all these crazy happenings."

"I know, right? Me, too. I just got off the phone with Olive Ramsey—"

"And I've decided that we shouldn't be investigating or writing about any of it anymore."

"What? Walt, what are you talking about?"

"Look, Nicole, this is some strange stuff. Dangerous stuff. We're in over our heads, don't you see? There are things at work here that maybe ordinary human beings shouldn't involve themselves in."

"Walt, look, I know this is some creepy shit. You don't think I'm—" then she caught herself. She wasn't going to say *scared*. "You don't think I'm concerned, too? But this article—it's going to be groundbreaking. We have proof that supernatural forces have been at work in this town. You're saying we should keep that to ourselves?"

"That's exactly what I'm saying. We've tapped into something that we need to walk away from, Nicole."

"Walt, come on, have a little courage."

"Courage, Nicole? Ten people are dead. You've been trying to convince me all along that their deaths are connected. Well, I'm convinced. This town has been in the grip of something we can't possibly understand and have no business even trying. And yet you want to mess with it? You want to write about it? You're tempting the devil, Nicole."

"Walt, would you listen to yourself? Look, I think we have a responsibility to the community. People need to know. Besides, can't you see that this is an article that media outlets all over the country are going to pick up? This is going to make us famous. Walt, this is Pulitzer Prize stuff!"

"Nicole, I'm sorry, I've made my decision. I know you're going to be upset with me and if you want to yell and cuss and storm out of here, well that's your prerogative. But we're dropping this one. The

New Liberty Gazette will not be handling this story. Period."

Walt stood, turned, and strode back into his office.

Nicole stormed after him. "That's fine, Walt. Walk away from everything! But you won't see me walking away. And you know what Dr. Ramsey just told me? The evil is now aware of my presence. That's right—my life might be in jeopardy, but you don't see me cowering in fear! I'm going to write this goddamned story, with your approval or not!"

Walt stood at his door, turned toward Nicole, and said softly, "Leave it alone, Nicole." Then he went inside his office, closing the door behind him.

Nicole stood for a moment, gathered herself together, and went back to her desk. Then she turned toward her laptop and continued working on the story that she knew she had to write, the story that was bigger than Walt and the *New Liberty Gazette*, the story that was going to put Nicole Anders on the map.

17

"**S**he said she's coming right in. I expect her here shortly." Debra Jennings called Nicole right after lunch. Nicole had spent the morning working on the article, lying to Walt who thought she was working on the marina renovation story. Earlier, she'd quickly dashed off a few paragraphs on the rash of burglaries and sent them to Walt's computer in an attempt to make him believe she'd dropped the consignment shop piece, but whether he believed it, she couldn't say. In fact, she started to think that by staying in the office and working, by not storming out as he'd expected, maybe she'd misplayed her hand. But if he was at all suspicious, he didn't let on. Maybe, she decided, Walt didn't really want to know what she was working on.

"Okay, thanks, Debra. I'll be there shortly." Nicole hung up and closed her laptop. "Walt, I'm going out for a bit," she called out as she made for the front door. "I'm heading to the marina to get a quote from the harbormaster for the story." Walt grunted something that sounded like approval and Nicole walked out the door.

She got in her Jeep and drove the three blocks to the consignment shop, calling Donnie along the way to tell him about the conversation she'd had with Dr. Ramsey and the plan to have her perform the dispersal ritual.

"You mean I need to swipe the candles *again?*" Donnie asked.

"Yes, but this is for the last time," Nicole said.

"I don't know, Nicole…"

"Donnie, you have to. Those candles present a real danger."

"But eventually someone will notice they're gone."

"Well…replace them with some others. Jordan's Gifts and Notions on Hilltop Avenue has candles just like them. Come on, Donnie. Nobody will notice because there's nothing left to investigate with the Horton house fire. There's no reason for anyone to ever look at that evidence bin again."

Finally, Donnie agreed and the two made plans to get together at Nicole's the next day and then go see Dr. Ramsey.

Nicole pulled into a parking spot across from the consignment shop and waited patiently, watching through the rearview mirror. At last, a woman pulled up to the front of the shop in an SUV. Probably in her early fifties, the woman, tall and slim with long, dirty-blond hair, got out of her car and strode into the shop with purpose. Nicole realized it must be Elaine, the owner of the items in booth 15.

Nicole waited a minute or two and then got out of her Jeep. She walked across the street and casually ambled into the store, throwing a nod at Debra, and then pretending to be a shopper. Elaine, meanwhile, was busy loading up a box with her possessions.

"I just don't understand why people are returning these things," she was saying to Debra. "They're all in such good condition."

"I know, and I'm sorry," Debra said. "All I can tell you is that the retail biz can be very unpredictable. Do you need another couple boxes?"

"Would you mind?"

"Not at all. Let me get them for you."

Debra went behind the counter and grabbed two more corrugated boxes. Elaine made a trip outside to her SUV with her first box, then came back in and filled the two additional ones.

Nicole sensed her chance. "Do you need help with one of those?" she said.

"Oh, thank you, I'd appreciate that."

Debra held the door open and Elaine and Nicole, each with a box, left the store.

Booth 15 was now empty.

Out in front of the store, Elaine opened the hatch-back and shoved her box into the back. Nicole set hers down beside it. She remembered the promise she'd made to Debra. She couldn't let on that Debra had told her about Elaine.

"You've got some interesting things here," she said. "I come into this shop from time to time and I noticed that your booth always had some really unique items."

"Well, thank you," said Elaine. "If there's anything you want—"

"Like, one time I saw some interesting bookends," Nicole continued. "Gargoyle bookends."

"Sure, I remember those. I guess *those* didn't get returned."

"Well, I was just wondering...where did you find all this stuff?"

"Hmm...I don't know. Just odds and ends I picked up over the years, I guess. No one place in particular. Why do you ask?"

Nicole hesitated, then decided that she had to tell her what she knew. Elaine had the right to know about the objects. She said it straight out. "Ma'am, did you know that the bookends were used in a murder?"

Elaine froze. "Huh? What are you talking about?"

"Do you remember the killings at the university this summer?

"The two college kids?"

"Yes."

"What are you saying?"

"The third girl, the murderer, she beat her room-mates to death with those bookends."

Elaine turned pale. "How do you know this?"

"I saw the police report. I'm a reporter with the *Gazette*."

"Well, why are you telling me this?"

"You need to know about the nature of the items that are in these boxes."

Elaine started walking around the side of the car toward the driver's side door, eyes looking straight down. "Listen, I really need to be going."

Nicole pressed on. "The flameless candles? Did you know they were found at the scene of that housefire that killed two people?"

"I'm sorry, I'm running late," Elaine said, opening the driver door and sliding inside.

"And the fireplace poker, and the dog leash, and the oil painting of the sailboats..."

Elaine tried to close the door but Nicole wedged herself in between.

"I have to go!" Elaine cried out.

"Ma'am," Nicole said, "whatever you do, please do not take these items into your house. Don't you see? There's evil in these boxes." Then Nicole moved aside. Elaine shut the door, threw the vehicle into reverse, and was soon roaring down the street. Nicole pulled out her phone and took a picture of the rear of the car as it sped away.

She doesn't believe me, Nicole thought to herself. In her mind, she'd imagined somehow having a rational conversation with Elaine. In retrospect, that seemed hopelessly naïve. This hadn't gone at all as she'd expected. *She thinks I'm batshit crazy. And why wouldn't she?*

Later that afternoon, Nicole enlarged the photo on her phone, noted the license number of the SUV, and looked it up in her database. Elaine Wilson lived at 278 Everglade Drive, about fifteen miles outside of town. Nicole waited until after dark then drove out to the subdivision where Elaine lived. She found Everglade and parked about fifty yards down from the Wilson house. Then she walked up the other side of the street, getting herself just close enough to the SUV to see, from the lamppost under which the vehicle was parked, that the boxes from the consignment shop were sitting in the back exactly where Elaine had packed them. She'd left them in the car. She hadn't taken them into the house. Interesting, thought Nicole. For whatever reason, maybe Elaine believed her after all.

The pendulum belonged to Luna. Apparently, it had been her grandmother's and Luna had come into possession of it upon her death. She knew very little about the pendulum. Her grandmother had rarely spoken of it, except to suggest that, in the right hand, it could be used for fortune telling. Only her grandmother didn't use the phrase "fortune telling." She called it "divination."

Whether Luna's grandmother really believed what she said, Luna never knew. Her grandmother had originally come from Latvia, the daughter of parents who were nomadic gypsies. Apparently, the pendulum had at one time belonged to Luna's great grandmother who had boasted of its powers. All Luna knew about it was that she liked the feel of it. It fit in the palm of her hand, was heavy crystal, cone-shaped, and it hung off the end of a foot-long gold chain.

Elaine Wilson sat in her chair by the window, remembering when Luna had brought the pendulum over to the house. Luna was the best friend of Elaine's daughter Cara. This was their senior year of high school and the girls were always together, typically hanging out with two other friends, Lauren and Valerie. Luna had shown the pendulum to Elaine. One day after school, all four girls were over. It was a common occurrence. The girls had enrolled in an after-school yoga class and they always came back to Cara's afterward. On this day, Luna had brought her pendulum along. "Check it out, Mrs. Wilson," she'd said to Elaine. "It was my grandmother's. She used to say you could tell the future with it." Then the girls had all gone down to the basement from where Elaine could hear lots of chattering and giggling.

Nobody was giggling anymore.

Elaine thought about what the reporter had told her in front of the consignment shop that afternoon. She had the TV on, tuned to some travel show, but she couldn't focus on it. She hadn't been able to focus on anything since coming home from the shop. Thankfully, Cara was at her father's for the night. Elaine couldn't have handled talking to Cara that evening. She couldn't even handle making herself dinner. She'd popped a frozen pizza into the microwave, then opened a much-needed bottle of wine. She was now on her third glass. The only light in the living room was the glow from the TV and through the blinds, Elaine could see her SUV. The boxes were in the back. What in God's name was she going to do with them? She sure as hell wasn't going to bring them into the house, that much was certain.

She thought back to that night when Luna had brought over the pendulum. The girls had found a website that gave advice on how divination pendulums work. You rest your elbow on a table and the pendulum hangs down and makes movements as you ask it questions. But you have to bond with the pendulum first, the website had suggested. To get yourself in tune with it. Oh, of course, it was all in good fun, but Luna took it seriously enough to start carrying the pendulum around with her twenty-four hours a day. Supposedly, after a while, you come to understand your pendulum's movements, which direction it swings for "yes," and which direction it swings for "no." Every evening that week, the girls got together in Elaine's basement to ask the pendulum questions. Elaine found it amusing. The girls were having fun and it was certainly better than having them out somewhere getting into trouble. Not that she had to worry about that. All four of the girls were straight-A students whose biggest offenses were sometimes breaking curfew.

Then one day Lauren had suggested they get a pendulum board. Elaine learned that a board provides more specific answers. You dangle the pendulum over it and the pendulum points to boxes on the board marked with letters and numbers in addition to "yes" and "no." The girls thought it was a great idea and Lauren found a board online, an old wooden one, explaining that she liked it precisely because it was old. "Who knows who might have used this in the past!" she'd said, wide-eyed. "Or for what reasons!"

The board arrived at Lauren's one day and that very night the girls all gathered in the basement to try it out. Elaine was upstairs, sitting at the kitchen table paying bills and trying to balance her checkbook. At one point, she noticed that the usual chattering and giggling had stopped. Things were quiet, strangely so. Then she heard a couple of audible gasps. She thought she heard one of the girls softly mutter, "Oh...my...God!" but she couldn't be sure. Ten minutes later, the girls all came upstairs.

"What was going on down there?" Elaine had asked. "You girls look like you've seen a ghost."

Nobody said a word until Valerie finally jumped in and said, "Oh, nothing Mrs. Wilson. We were just fooling around. You know."

Then Cara's friends all left. Cara said something about getting some homework done and retreated to her bedroom, closing the door behind her.

With curiosity getting the better of her, Elaine went downstairs, not knowing what she was expecting to see. She flicked the light on. Nothing seemed out of the ordinary. Lauren had left the board on the card table, but Luna had apparently taken the pendulum with her. Nothing was out of place.

Then she saw the boxes that she'd stacked in the corner of the room and remembered that she had to take them to the consignment shop. A month before, she'd done a heavy spring cleaning and had decided that this was going to be the year she got rid of all the junk she didn't need, boxing up various items with the idea that maybe she could make a few bucks selling them. "A consignment shop?" Cara had said when Elaine had mentioned it. "Mom, this is the twenty-first century. Why don't you just sell them on eBay?" Old-school when it came to making financial transactions, Elaine had decided she was satisfied with the consignment shop idea. Looking at the boxes, she made a note to take them out to the car the next day, walked back up the steps, and flicked the light off behind her.

Everything seemed normal the following day. Elaine and Cara had breakfast together before Cara went off to school and nothing was said about the goings-on in the basement the night before. Elaine didn't get around to taking the boxes out to the car that day and so they were still there that evening when the girls all came over after yoga and went back down to the basement.

Again, Elaine noticed the lack of laughter and general merriment she'd come to expect from the gatherings of her daughter and her daughter's friends. The activities down in the basement were apparently serious, whatever they were. Later that night, she'd find out why. After Luna, Valerie, and Lauren had all gone home, Elaine asked Cara about the basement doings.

"What's going on down there, anyway?" she said. "Are you still playing around with that pendulum thing?"

Cara was quiet for a moment and then, as if to unburden herself, proceeded to tell her mother that, yes, they were still experimenting with Luna's pendulum. "But, Mom, something strange started happening once Lauren brought over that board. You're supposed to hold the pendulum over it, right? And then the pendulum makes slight movements toward the little boxes with the answers to whatever questions you ask. Luna holds the pendulum because she's the one in tune with it. I mean, that's the way it's supposed to work, anyway. But, Mom, the pendulum moves really weirdly over that board."

"What do you mean 'weirdly'?" Elaine had asked.

"Like, erratically. It doesn't swing or sway. It jerks, and it jerks all over the place. It's like the pendulum doesn't want to point to anything on the board at all."

Elaine smiled. "Are you sure that's not Luna moving it like that? You know her sense of humor."

"Mom," Cara said, turning even more serious, "last night, the pendulum pointed straight out to the side."

"What do you mean?"

"I mean, parallel with the table. As though it was being pulled. It was defying gravity, Mom. It was the single most freaky thing I've ever seen."

"Look, Cara, maybe you guys shouldn't play around with it anymore. I'm sure there's a simple enough explanation, but if it's freaking you all out, then maybe you should give it a rest. Besides, finals are coming up, right? You girls ought to be spending more time studying."

"Yeah, I guess so," Cara had said.

"You know, when I was in high school, my friends and I played with a Ouija board. Sometimes you can let your imagination get the better of you with those kinds of things. Looking back now as an adult, I can see how silly it was."

Cara had nodded in apparent agreement, but Elaine honestly didn't know what to make of the story Cara had related to her. Ultimately, she put it down to the overactive imagination of four high school girls. Someone thought they'd seen something strange and, through the unintentional power of suggestion, all the girls had come to believe it. A microcosmic example of mass hysteria, perhaps. Elaine remembered studying about it in a psychology class in college. Still, she found the episode a bit unnerving. She had to admit that when she'd first seen that board, it had strangely creeped her out, though she couldn't say exactly why.

The next evening, to Elaine's dismay, the girls reconvened in the basement once more. Well, maybe it was for the best, Elaine thought. Maybe tonight nothing strange happens and everyone can go home and move beyond the whole thing. The pendulum and pendulum board will become nothing more than a passing fancy.

From upstairs, Elaine would not be witness to what went on in the basement that night. Had she been downstairs with the girls, she would have seen them sitting around the card table with the pendulum and board as on prior nights, but this time bathed in candlelight. The candles were Luna's idea. "It says online that the light from candles can cleanse the board," she explained. She'd brought incense, too, another means, so she'd learned, by which to rid the environment of any malevolent spirits.

"Okay, well let's get on with it," Cara said. "My mom doesn't even want us to be down here."

"I'm not sure *I* even want to be down here," said Valerie. "All this shit is starting to creep me out."

"Come on, Luna," said Lauren, "get us started."

"Okay," Luna said, and then, with her elbow on the table, she dangled the pendulum over the board. "What should I ask it?"

She glanced around at her friends. The glow from the candles placed around the board was casting strange shadows over their faces.

"We need to ask who's been guiding the pendulum," said Lauren. "Who's the spirit behind what's been happening?"

"I don't know, guys," said Valerie. "Maybe we shouldn't..."

"Come on, Val," said Lauren. "We talked about this. We all need to be on board or it won't work."

"Okay, okay. But I'm telling you, this is the last time for me."

"Go, Luna," said Cara. "Focus, everyone."

Luna took a deep breath. "Spirit, can you hear me?"

Several seconds elapsed. The pendulum hung motionless.

"Spirit," she repeated, "can you hear me?"

Imperceptibly at first, then unmistakably, the pendulum began to swing in a straight line left and right, along the axis that designated a negative response.

"It's saying 'no,' Lauren whispered. "How could that be?"

"It's toying with us," said Cara.

"Luna, you better not be screwing with us," said Valerie.

"How can I be? Look at my fingers. I'm not moving."

Then the pendulum stopped. Immediately. Completely.

The girls gasped.

Then, in a moment, the pendulum began swinging wildly about the board. And then it did something it hadn't before. It swung in a vertical loop, twice around Luna's fingers and then it rose straight upwards, pointing directly toward the ceiling, 180 degrees away from the board. Terrified, none of the girls could move nor speak.

Then the board began to shake. And then the table. It seemed to the girls as if the room itself was soon quaking.

Cara saw it first. The boxes Elaine had stacked in the corner were beginning to sway. And then in an instant, as if someone were behind the boxes giving the stack a violent shove, the boxes all came flying down, crashing to the floor.

Elaine heard the crash and witnessed the rest, the girls screaming and racing up the basement steps. She went down to find the source of the noise, flipping the light switch on and discovering that the stack of boxes filled with the items slated for the consignment shop had been knocked over. Now the items were scattered all over the floor. She ran back upstairs where the girls were standing, all pale and trembling.

"What happened down there?" Elaine demanded to know. "Who knocked over my boxes of stuff?"

"Nobody," Cara said breathlessly. "They just came tumbling down, Mom. Honest to God!"

Elaine had had enough. "Okay, that's it!" she told the girls. "No more of this pendulum stuff. I don't care how the boxes fell, I want you girls to go down there and pick everything up. And throw that damn board in with all the other stuff. Lauren, I'm sorry, I'll reimburse you for whatever you paid for it, but I'm not going to have you guys continue to come here and freak yourselves out. You've all got much better things to do with your time."

The girls looked around at each other, none daring to move.

"You heard me," Elaine said. "Get everything picked up. And after you've re-boxed everything, take the boxes out to my car. I'm taking all of that junk to the consignment shop first thing in the morning. Including the board!"

Later that night, Elaine searched online for information about pendulums and pendulum boards. All she knew was what Cara had told her. She visited several sites and came away with a little more understanding about them but it didn't necessarily make her feel any better. Based on the sources she found, the general idea seemed to be that the pendulum and board work together to convey messages "from the spirit world." Elaine had never been one for that kind of thing and, under other circumstances, might have dismissed the whole idea as silly. But there was something very sincere and genuine in the descriptions she'd found. People believed this stuff. Apparently, lots of people. The girls certainly did. Elaine could not forget the petrified looks on their faces as they raced up the steps from the basement. Could there be something to it all?

And now, months later, from her chair in the living room, Elaine looked again out of the window at her SUV and felt with a shiver as if maybe she had her answer. The boxes were back in her possession. And she knew the board was in there, too. Nothing more had ever been said about the whole pendulum thing but Elaine could not forget what the girls had claimed they'd seen. What had happened that last night in the basement? She never did ask Cara. If she were honest with herself, she didn't really want to know.

Then came that reporter at the consignment shop, revealing to her the common denominator of all of those strange murders and accidents she'd read about all summer. The common denominator was that the people involved had all come into possession of her items. It was as if they'd been tainted in some way. Now the returns made sense.

That board. That damn pendulum board.

Elaine poured herself another glass of wine, turned off the TV, and sat in the dark, periodically glancing outside at the car, wondering just exactly what evil

had been wrought in her basement and where, if anywhere, it would all end.

19

Nicole had asked for the weekend off and Walt had been good enough to give it to her. She'd sent him a draft of the marina renovation piece and he'd seemed satisfied that her focus was now back where it belonged. Or maybe he'd only convinced himself it was back where it belonged. Nicole couldn't tell. Truthfully, it had become their own little version of "Don't ask, don't tell." He hadn't asked anymore about her plans to do any further investigating of the consignment shop items, and she hadn't volunteered anything.

It was Saturday morning and Donnie was expected at any moment. Nicole glanced around the house one more time to make sure it was presentable, then checked the bathroom mirror one more time to make sure she was as well. Not that she was trying to impress Donnie in any way. Donnie wasn't her type. There was nothing wrong with being a fireman, of course, but she'd always seen herself with someone more...cerebral. Maybe a professor. Or perhaps a doctor. She'd imagined herself in New York working for the *Times*, walking into a cocktail party in some swanky Manhattan apartment, maybe the home of a famous author or celebrity. She needed someone on her arm who made a sophisticated, urbane impression. Nevertheless, vanity prevented her from being cavalier about her or her home's appearance, even if it was just Donnie Olson from New Liberty High she was expecting.

The night before, she'd called Dr. Ramsey again. She explained about booth 15 in the consignment shop. Would it be enough, Nicole had asked, for them to destroy just the candles? Or would they have to destroy each and every item? Nicole knew the answer before she asked the question, but without actually breaking into Elaine Wilson's car and stealing the boxes, what could they do?

Of course Dr. Ramsey had confirmed her suspicions. "Nicole, every object that has spent any time at all with those candles needs to be destroyed."

Nicole asked her what "any time at all" meant.

"Look for the common denominator, Nicole," Dr. Ramsey answered. "There is something in particular that has infected those items, and at a particular moment in time. It's called 'demonic contagion.' Now, maybe it's the candles themselves that did the infecting, who can say? But some single item in that consignment store booth is the source item. Most likely, the source item was somehow exposed to tremendous evil at some point in the past. And then, through some supernatural occurrence—an inciting event, if you will—the source item infected the items in its immediate surroundings. Now each item is as infested as the source item. Do you see? And so every item needs to be destroyed."

"What would have been the inciting event?" Nicole asked.

"It could be anything. The source item is a conduit, right? That makes it dangerous in and of itself. But sometimes, evil can be encouraged to find it, to be invited in. Like through a séance, maybe, or perhaps through incantation. My guess is that sometime recently, someone, intentionally or unintentionally, did something to summon evil upon the source object, more evil than what it was already carrying. This allowed for the demonic contagion of the rest of the items."

"I see."

"Now, listen, Nicole, come here with the candles as planned tomorrow. We'll do the ritual and then you'll know how to do it yourself."

"Me?"

"Yes, Nicole. You're going to have to repeat the ritual for every item that was in that consignment shop booth."

"Okay, Dr. Ramsey. I understand."

Nicole had thanked her and hung up, wondering what she was going to do about those damn boxes, how to get Elaine to part with them, imagining herself trying to explain specter dispersal and demonic contagion. Finally, she'd decided that she'd just show up on Elaine's doorstep with Donnie and try to reason with her. But she knew that what she'd have to explain to Elaine was surely going to sound like the most *un*reasonable thing Elaine had ever heard.

Donnie rang the bell right on time. Nicole waved him inside. "Do you have them?"

Donnie opened up his small duffel bag and showed them to Nicole. "There they are," he said. "You should see the replacements. Identical. Nobody's ever going to be the wiser."

"See? I told you."

"So what now?"

"Well, like I said, we're going to take them to Dr. Ramsey. We need to break them apart first? Any ideas?"

"Sure, I have a vice on the bed of my truck outside. We can squeeze them in there and they'll explode into bits."

"Okay, that sounds good. Then, after Dr. Ramsey's, we can swing by Elaine Wilson's place."

"Whose place?"

"Elaine Wilson. She's the woman who owned the candles. The one with all the consignment shop items.

I drove to her house last night. Everything is in boxes in her car outside of her house. We have to convince her to let us help her destroy everything."

"How are we going to do that?"

"Great question."

"She's going to think we're nuts."

"Maybe. But when I approached her yesterday afternoon, she seemed kind of spooked and skittish. I don't know...I had the impression she knew more about those items than she let on. And then she left them in her car, right? Why did she do that?"

"But, Nicole, even if she thinks there's something wrong with the stuff that's in those boxes, she would never just allow us to take the things and promise to destroy them. She doesn't even know who we are."

"Well, she knows I'm with the *Gazette*. You tell her you're with the fire department. Show her some ID. Who's more trustworthy than a first responder?"

"But even still, she can't admit that her stuff is cursed. Can you imagine if that were to get out? The publicity and everything?"

Actually, Nicole had imagined it. As a matter of fact, it *was* going to get out. It would all go into the article. But of course nobody, including Donnie, needed to know that at this point. "Well, Donnie, we have to try, don't we? Every one of those boxed items is a ticking time bomb. Now come on, time's wasting.

Let's make use of that vice of yours and pulverize these fucking things."

Out in front of Nicole's place, Donnie climbed up onto the bed of his pickup and placed one of the candles between the jaws of his vice. He turned the handle but when the jaws clamped around the candle, he could turn no further. He grunted, twisting the handle as hard as he could but the vice's sliding jaw refused to budge.

"What's wrong?" Nicole asked.

"I don't know. Damn thing won't break."

"Shit. Try the other one."

Donnie removed the first candle and placed the second one in the vice. Again, he turned the handle as hard as he could.

"*Goddamn!*" he said. Then, with all his might, he twisted the handle once more. This time the candle cracked and then shattered.

At that moment, Nicole heard the squeal of tires and the screeching of brakes. She looked up just in time to see a car careening down the road in front of the house, the driver desperately wrestling with the steering wheel, swerving around Donnie's truck, barely missing it, before coming to a stop at Nicole's mailbox, knocking it over in the process.

"What the fuck?!" Donnie exclaimed from the bed of the truck.

A man, clearly shaken, got out of the car. "Holy shit," he said, his face white. "I can't believe that just happened. It was like the fucking steering wheel seemed to turn on its own!" He took a couple of deep breaths, collected himself, and assessed the damage. Turning to Nicole and Donnie, he said, "Is this your house?"

"It's mine," Nicole said. "And so is the mailbox. Or was."

"Jesus, I'm sorry as hell," the man said. "Wow, I mean, I don't know what happened. The car just sort of got away from me, I guess."

"Are you okay?"

"Yeah, I just need to catch my breath. I'll pay for your mailbox, of course. Damn, I'm sorry."

Donnie jumped down from the bed and took a look at the mailbox. "Yeah, it's pretty totaled."

"Here's my card," the man said, handing his business card to Nicole. "Call me with the damages and I'll send you a check." Then the man, still breathing hard, apologized again and slowly drove off.

Donnie turned to Nicole. "Nicole, we have a term we use down at the firehouse. FUBAR. Fucked Up

Beyond All Recognition. If you ask me, this whole thing is FUBAR."

"What do you mean?"

"What do I mean? That guy lost control of his car at the exact moment I broke the second candle and he almost slammed into us. You don't find that FUBAR?"

"Donnie, this shit is fucked up, I admit, but that was just a coincidence. It's a busy road. It's not the first time a car has veered onto the sidewalk."

"That's bullshit, Nicole, and you know it."

"He didn't even hit us. He hit the mailbox."

"Which could have just as easily been us! Nicole, you're starting to worry me. You've become so obsessed by your story that I don't think you understand the magnitude of the danger. We got lucky. *This* time."

"Well, look, Donnie, we broke the candle, okay? We're doing what Dr. Ramsey advised, right?"

"We broke *one* of them. Nicole, these things are plastic. I should be able to break this candle by stepping on it. I'm telling you, this is *fucked up*."

"Okay, well, we'll take the candles to Dr. Ramsey. Come on. We'll call her on our way. She'll know what to do."

"I sure as hell hope so." Donnie grabbed the first candle and the pieces of the second, muttering under his breath, "FUBAR. This is so fucking FUBAR."

"I was afraid of something like this."

Nicole had Dr. Ramsey on speaker phone in the car.

"What do you mean, Doctor?"

"It's the same kind of taunt as with my burned hands. It's the evil showing off again. It allows you to break one candle, but not the other. You see? It's toying with you. Now, bring everything to me as soon as you can, Nicole. Let's get this taken care of."

"Okay. We're on our way."

Nicole hung up.

"So you heard her," Donnie said. "You still think the car totaling your mailbox was a fucking coincidence, Nicole!?"

But Nicole stared straight ahead and said nothing.

"We drive you from us, whoever you may be, unclean spirits, all satanic powers. As the inferno is over, the smoke is driven away; forever buried is where you will stay."

Nicole's eyes were supposed to be closed, but she couldn't help peeking at Dr. Ramsey as Dr. Ramsey repeated the incantation over the glob of melted plastic. She and Donnie and Dr. Ramsey were seated on Dr. Ramsey's back deck in a circle, holding hands, eyes supposedly closed. Between them, on a tile table, was a metal pan where half the pieces from the first shattered candle had been burned and melted. Soon, they would do the other half.

Donnie had poured lighter fluid on the pieces and lit the flame. Dr. Ramsey answered the question that was on everybody's mind. "See?" she said. "Once broken, the evil loses its dominion. That's why they'll burn now where they didn't before."

Nicole was jotting it all down in her head. The smell of the burning plastic, the calm, focused look on Dr. Ramsey's face as she repeated the incantation, the scared look on Donnie's—it was all going to go in the article.

The article. That's what was keeping Nicole focused. If she allowed herself to think about what they were really doing—performing some sort of occult ritual over the remains of an ordinary item that had somehow been held in dominion by a demonic force that was responsible for the gruesome deaths of people—if she allowed herself to think about that, well, she imagined she'd look like Donnie, pale as a ghost and creeped out beyond reason.

The ritual was repeated for the other half of the remains and, after cooling, each half was relegated to a tin coffee can.

"Okay," said Dr. Ramsey, "I think you'll find that the other candle will break now."

Donnie placed the candle on the table and struck it with a hammer that Dr. Ramsey had provided. Easily, it cracked into two pieces. He struck it again. And again. Each time, it broke into further pieces.

"Wow," was all Donnie could say.

"The evil is gone," said Dr. Ramsey, smiling. "The candles were a pair. Individually, they have no power. Just the same, put half the pieces on the pan and use the lighter fluid. Just like the first one. We'll take no chances."

The ritual, including the incantation was repeated for one half of the pieces, then the other half. Two more globs of melted plastic were dropped into two more coffee cans.

"You know what to do now," said Dr. Ramsey.

"Yes, ma'am," Donnie replied. "I brought a shovel. We'll bury these a couple of miles apart, like you said."

"Nicole," Dr. Ramsey said, "I'll write the incantation down for you. Do you have any questions about what we did here today?"

"I don't think so."

"When will you be retrieving the other items?"

"Soon, Dr. Ramsey."

"It can't be soon enough."
"I understand."

It was a haggard-looking Elaine Wilson who answered the door that morning. She'd barely slept and was nursing a headache from the bottle of wine of the night before. Seeing Nicole from the *New Liberty Gazette* on her doorstep didn't do much to make her feel better.

"Hi, Ms. Wilson," Nicole began, "I hate to bother you, but we really need to talk about the items from the consignment shop."

"Listen, miss..."

"Nicole. Nicole Anders. And this is my friend Donnie Olson from the New Liberty Fire Department."

"Pleased to meet you, ma'am," Donnie said.

Elaine gave a curt nod, then turned to Nicole and said, "Ms. Anders, I really don't know what to tell you. I don't know anything about those items. I had them lying around for a while, boxed them up, took them to the consignment shop, and then brought them home when they didn't sell. I don't understand why they are of so much interest to you."

"I couldn't help but notice that you left them in the back of your vehicle."

"Well, I...I just haven't had a chance to bring them in."

"I'm going to be straight with you, Ms. Wilson. I think you know more about the items than you're letting on. Now, Donnie here happened to be on duty the night of the fire that killed that young couple. Do you remember the flameless candles of yours? They were there. In the front window where the fire started. Tell her, Donnie."

"Well," Donnie said, "the thing is, ma'am, those candles emerged from the fire in perfect shape. Like they were brand new."

"Right," Nicole said, "and I already told you about the gargoyle bookends. And—"

"Look, Ms. Anders, if you're somehow saying that I'm in any way responsible for any of the terrible tragedies this town has endured over the summer—"

"Oh, no, Ms. Wilson. No, no, no. We're not saying that at all. But we are saying that, as bizarre and unbelievable as it might sound, there's something wrong with the stuff that's in those boxes of yours. Now, I've consulted with an expert on supernatural forces and..." Nicole paused. "Ms. Wilson, may we please come in?"

Elaine hesitated, then seemed to resign herself to the idea that Nicole Anders of the *New Liberty Gazette* was not going to go away. She sighed. "Okay, but I have things to do."

"We promise we won't stay long."

"Come in," Elaine said, ushering Nicole and Donnie into the living room.

Once seated, Nicole continued. "Have you ever heard of demonic infestation, Ms. Wilson?"

Elaine shook her head.

"It's when an inanimate object becomes, well, for lack of a better word, possessed by an evil force. In technical terms, the force holds what's called 'dominion' over the article. Any object can become...infected, so to speak. Often times it happens through what's called demonic contagion. Through some inciting event where evil spirits are conjured up, like a séance or something, an evil item can spread its evil nature to other items."

Even as she spoke, Nicole wondered how anybody could believe her. But to her surprise, Elaine Wilson didn't seem especially skeptical. In fact, a sort of strange expression came over her face when Nicole mentioned the idea of a séance. Nicole continued speaking at length about what she'd learned from Dr. Ramsey, about the summer deaths, and about the possible role of the consignment shop items.

Finally, she circled back to the inciting event concept. "Can you think of anything that might have happened with the articles in those boxes, Ms. Wilson? Anything at all?"

Elaine was quiet for a long moment. At last, she replied, "No, not really. I mean, well, a few months ago my daughter and some of her friends were down in the basement where I had everything boxed up. And one night..."

"Yes?"

"Well, it's really nothing Ms. Anders. They're just kids, you know? One of them brought over a pendulum board and they got to fooling around with it, that's all. But nothing really happened."

"Well, something must have happened, Ms. Wilson."

Elaine shook her head and suddenly stood. "Like I said, it was nothing. Now, Ms. Anders, if you'll excuse me, I really have a lot to do today." Then she walked toward the door, opening it for Nicole and Donnie, signifying the end of her patience and the meeting.

Nicole and Donnie exchanged glances and then rose and followed Elaine to the door.

"Ms. Wilson," Nicole said on her way out, "is your daughter around? If you could just allow me to talk to her for two minutes—"

"Certainly not, Ms. Anders! She's just a young girl. All this talk of demons and evil spirits is ridiculous and I won't subject my daughter to it! Now, I'm sorry I can't be of more help, but you really need to be going. I have a lot to do today."

"Ms. Wilson, if you would just allow us to take the boxes—"

But Nicole found herself on the front porch speaking to a closed door.

"Damn," she said, turning to Donnie. "That woman knows more. She knows a *lot* more."

20

It was the third showing in as many days. This time it was a young couple who were moving into the area from Ohio. The husband had been transferred and the wife was pregnant and they both seemed very interested in the house on Everglade Drive.

Elaine had put the house up for sale just a week after she'd retrieved the boxes from the consignment shop. It was something she'd been considering for a while. After the divorce, the place just hadn't seemed the same. Too many bad memories. She knew it would only get worse when Cara went off to college and she'd be left all alone in the house. And then, of course, well, there was the basement. Elaine hadn't gone down there since the reporter from the *Gazette* had stopped by that Saturday morning with all that talk about demons and evil spirits. She knew she'd be lying to herself to say that the basement didn't factor into the decision.

Nevertheless, basement or no basement, it was time to move on and, five minutes away, she'd found the cutest little condo. It was just a small two-bedroom, but it was modern, with all new appliances and everything. And the building had a pool and a gym. Of course Elaine had to downsize, so that meant putting a lot of her stuff into storage. Including those damn boxes from the consignment shop. She didn't know how much to believe of what the reporter had said. She'd come back saying something about destroying all the objects, but Elaine wasn't interested in hearing about any of it. Why couldn't she just leave her alone? Anyway, there was no way she was bringing those boxes into her home again. What she would ultimately do with them, she had no idea. For now, they were in a storage unit and that was good enough. Out of sight, out of mind.

Elaine had gone out to the backyard while the Realtor, Tanya, a personal friend of hers, had taken today's couple on a tour of the home. She was sitting at the picnic table, idly scrolling through the newsfeed on her phone.

"I think they're going to make an offer!"

Elaine turned around to see Tanya coming out into the yard.

"Really?"

"Yes, they love it. They just left, but the husband said he was going to call me later today. But, listen, even if they don't, we're going to have no problem selling this house. I mean, look at the traffic we've had already."

"I know. Well, I hope we sell it soon. It's kind of a pain having to keep it so neat all the time!"

"Yes, about that, Elaine..."

"What?"

"Well...it's the basement."

"The basement? What about it?"

"It's just so...drafty and cold, you know? And dark. Even with the lights on. It's just not a very welcoming place. It's kind of creepy, to be honest with you and I hesitate to even take people down there. There's a bad vibe in that basement, you know? And an odd smell. Maybe some water got in somewhere. Do you think you can put a dehumidifier down there? And we can spray fabric spray on the furniture before the next showing. I have some scented candles that I sometimes use at open houses and people always comment about how great the houses smell. I'll bring one of those, too. And we should do something about the lighting. And you really ought to try to figure out where the draft is coming from. Has it always been like that? It must be freezing down there in the winter." Then Tanya smiled and turned to go. "Well, just let me know how I can help. I'll call you later today, hopefully with good news from this couple. Fingers crossed!"

"Here it is." Cara pulled out the pendulum board and handed it to Lauren. "I knew it was in one of these boxes. Are you sure you really want it? I'm still having nightmares about that night."

"I'm going to take it to State with me," Lauren replied. "Thinking about that night scares me too, Cara, but Luna and I really want to try using it again."

The two girls were in Elaine's storage unit. Lauren had allowed Elaine to box up her board, and even offer to pay for it, but Lauren never quite liked the idea of having it taken from her. She was relieved to hear that it hadn't sold in the consignment shop. When Cara had mentioned that, Lauren insisted that she be given the board back. She'd told Luna that she'd pick up the pendulum, too.

"Did I tell you that Luna wants to try to connect with her grandmother?" Lauren continued.

"The one who gave her the pendulum?"

"Yep. She's sure she can do it and I promised to help. By the way, we found a third roommate for our apartment. We Zoomed with her yesterday and she seems really sweet. We even like the same music. And we mentioned the pendulum thing and she was into it."

"I don't know what you guys see in it," Cara said. "It just feels evil."

"I'm not so sure, Cara. I look at it like this: where there's evil there's good, right? Two sides of the same coin. Now, the board is neutral. So maybe we tapped into evil that night because we weren't doing it right. Maybe we weren't taking it seriously enough or asking the right questions, you know? Luna and I are going to do more research and try to find a way to tap into the good that has to be out there. And trying to connect with her grandmother can only bring good things, wouldn't you think?"

"I guess. You guys be careful. I don't think you want to be fooling around with this stuff if you don't know what you're doing."

"We'll figure it out, Cara. Luna wants to be careful, too. Between you and me, I think she was just as shaken up as we were that night, even though she tries to come across as some mystic queen. So where's the pendulum?"

"I don't know. It doesn't seem to be here. Are you sure Luna doesn't have it?"

"Positive. She said she left it down in your basement. She hadn't seen it since it flew out of her hand that night."

"Well, I don't see it here."

"Let's go through the boxes again."

The two girls emptied the boxes of their contents and sifted through the items to no avail.

"It must still be in your basement," Lauren concluded.

"I don't remember seeing it anywhere."

"Well, who knows? Maybe it flew under the sofa or something. It's got to still be there."

"Yeah, I guess so."

"We've got to find it. Luna will freak out if we lost her grandmother's pendulum."

"I know, I know. Well, then I guess we need to go back to my house and look for it. Let's box this crap up and get going."

"What's your mom going to do with all this, anyway?"

"I don't know. She was disappointed it didn't sell. I wish I could help. With selling the house and everything, she's got so much on her mind. Maybe I'll figure a way to get rid of all of this stuff for her."

"Hey, whatever happened to those cool bookends she had? I wouldn't mind those. I could take them to State, too!"

"Apparently, those actually sold. Not much else did, though. Come on, let's go. If that pendulum is back in our basement, I'd like to find it and get it the hell out of there."

Elaine dragged the humidifier down the steps. The guy at the hardware store said it was their top-of-the-line unit before he rattled off a lot of specifications that meant nothing to Elaine—three-gallon capacity, thirty-six-hour runtime, auto shutoff, digital controls. It was on sale, that's what closed the deal for Elaine.

She looked for a place to put it and then noticed something strange. The basement didn't smell anymore. After Tanya had mentioned the smell, Elaine had gone down and noticed the smell right away. Cara had noticed it, too. And now it wasn't there at all. She couldn't seem to feel the cool draft, either. She walked around, sniffing, waving her hand around to feel for air movement. Everything seemed normal. The basement seemed just like it always had. If anything, it smelled fresh. It smelled clean.

She shrugged and walked back upstairs, noticing that Cara had come out of her bedroom and was in the kitchen fixing herself some breakfast. She'd slept in, just like she did every Sunday morning.

"Good morning, honey."

"Morning, Mom."

"Hey, Cara, you and Lauren were in the basement yesterday, weren't you?"

"Yep. Still smells down there, Mom," Cara replied, putting an overloaded spoonful of cereal in her mouth.

"Yeah, well, I bought a humidifier this morning and...Cara, did you and Lauren clean up or something?"

"Clean up? Hell, no, Mom. I just wanted to get out of there."

"Well, what were you doing down there?"

"Looking for Luna's pendulum. It wasn't in the boxes so we figured maybe it got left in the basement."

"Oh. Did you find it?"

"Yep. It was in the corner, right behind the sofa against the far wall where the boxes had been stacked up. No idea how it got there, but that whole night was a blur to me. Anyway, Lauren was going to take it to Luna, so it's out of there now, thank God. Anyway, it really smelled bad down there yesterday. Hope the humidifier works. The sooner we get out of here, the better. Well, I gotta go. I'm meeting Val and we're going to go look at prom dresses."

Cara put her empty bowl in the sink and walked out of the kitchen.

"Okay," Elaine managed to say. Then she stood silently in the kitchen for several minutes before she was finally able to convince herself that some things are coincidences and there's no reason to give them any further thought.

21

The move had gone well. Elaine felt like a new woman in the condo. And the couple from Ohio had purchased the house so that was a load off her mind. Cara loved the new condo, too. She had taken most of her stuff to college in the fall, but still decorated the condo's small second bedroom to her liking. And every other weekend, she came home.

There was, of course, the matter of all the junk in the storage unit. Elaine knew that, sooner or later, she'd have to deal with it. The storage unit cost money, after all. For the most part, however, Elaine didn't spend a lot of time thinking about it. Truthfully, she didn't want to. She had more or less blocked out the disturbing events that had occurred in her basement over the summer. That all happened months ago. Now it was early December. The Christmas season had arrived and the storage unit could wait. Maybe in the spring she'd be ready to deal with it. Maybe then she'd be ready to deal with those particular boxes that had been down in the basement, the boxes that held the objects that were…how did that reporter put it? Demonically infested? Something like that. Of course there was that comment about how the objects needed to be destroyed. What was that all about? Well, whatever. At least now, everything was boxed up and out of harm's way. Demonically infested or not, those items weren't going to hurt anybody locked away in the storage unit. And at least the reporter hadn't bothered her for a while, which was good. It was even better that she hadn't bothered Cara. The less Cara knew about everything, the better.

But on this particular weekend, Cara had come home and had some news to share with Elaine. Friday night, over a homemade pizza, she declared, "Mom, I have an early Christmas present for you!"

"Oh, yeah? What is it, honey?"

"Well, you know those boxes of junk in the storage unit?"

Elaine felt her heart skip a beat. "Yes?"

"I know how you've had all that stuff on your mind, wondering what you can do with all of it…"

"Yes?"

"And I know how much of a technophobe you are…"

"Cara, what are you saying?" Elaine forced a smile and tried to sound calm.

"Well, guess what? I sold everything on eBay! Isn't that great? It's all gone!"

Elaine felt faint.

Cara, caught up in her certain good news, didn't notice her mom's reaction. With a big smile, she continued. "I've been dying to tell you about it, but I wanted to wait until everything was sold first and surprise you!" She pulled a check out of her pants pocket. "Here! The money all came into my account, so here's a check. I didn't think I'd sell it all, but everything went. It was so much fun! The buyers were from all over. Isn't that crazy? Mom, you're not saying anything. You didn't want to keep all that crap, did you? Geez, I hope not!" Then she chuckled. "Well, I mean, it's too late now. Those old junk items are in homes all over the country! Mom? Mom, you look pale. Are you okay? What's the matter? Did I do something wrong?"

22

"Damn! Stupid fucking piece of shit!" Nicole pulled out the broken drinking glass, all three pieces of it, from the upper shelf of the dishwasher, careful not to cut her fingers on the sharp edges. She dropped the pieces into the garbage can then pulled out the lower shelf of the dishwasher to see if there were any shards that needed to be retrieved. It was the second time that week that something had broken in the dishwasher. Something was definitely wrong with it. Now she'd have to call the landlord and demand a new one. She liked the little one-bedroom house she rented close to town, but she hated having to deal with the old man that owned the place. It was like pulling teeth to ever get him to fix or replace anything. She could already hear him telling her that she must have loaded it wrong. As if it's rocket science to load a fucking dishwasher.

What was going to make it worse was that she'd had to call him just a few days before to report a crack in the sliding glass door. A week earlier, the whole area had been hit with a hard freeze, temperatures dipping below zero. The door had glazed with ice and after it had thawed, Nicole noticed a long hairline crack that was sure to get worse if she didn't get it taken care of. There was no telling when the glass would be replaced and until then, she'd have to live with a three-foot-long crack in the door and hope that the glass somehow held in place. And now she'd have to wash the dishes by hand for the foreseeable future.

Deep down, Nicole realized she didn't have any cause to complain. The house was one of the rare affordable ones this close to town. One had to expect some problems. All in all, it served her well. It was small but surprisingly bright and cheery, made more so by a skylight in the living room right above the sofa. The house had been built in the 1940s and the skylight was original. Rather than today's plexiglass, it was made of thick glass. There were times during especially heavy rains when Nicole could notice just a trace of moisture around the periphery of the skylight, and she wondered if it was beginning to somehow separate from the roof. If it ever fell in it would probably kill whoever might be sitting underneath it. But if it lasted this long, certainly it wasn't going to fail any time soon.

Nicole didn't find any more glass in the dishwasher—at least it broke cleanly, she thought—and she unloaded the rest of the dishes, deciding that that would be the last chore of the day. It was close to midnight and she was tired. She'd spent most of the day polishing up the story. Now, it was done. The next day, she'd present it to Walt. There was no way he could turn it down. She'd detailed everything. She had traced the route of the consignment shop items from the shop to the homes of each person who'd been tragically killed. Furthermore, she'd interviewed Dr. Olive Ramsey at length and devoted several paragraphs to the concept of demonic possession, using other examples from the field of parapsychology. Finally, she had detailed the ritual they had performed over the candles.

If there had been one loose end it was the tracing of the objects from Elaine Wilson's house. Yes, they all came from Elaine, but what had happened to them before they were delivered to the shop? Something, obviously. She'd gone back to interview Elaine again, and to press upon her the need for the items to be destroyed, offering to do it, but this time, Elaine refused to open the door more than a crack. "I've told you all I know," she'd said. "And I don't want to hear anything more about demons."

Nicole had noticed the boxes were no longer in Elaine's SUV out front and when she asked about them, Elaine told her they'd been put in storage. She was going to be moving. Then she'd shut the door. Meanwhile, Elaine's daughter had gone off to college somewhere, so that turned out to be a dead-end, too. Finally, Nicole decided to finish the article with what she had. The origin of the evil would remain a mystery, but didn't that make the whole matter even more intriguing? The article was complete and if Walt didn't want to publish it, then screw him. She'd quit and take the piece elsewhere. It was a brilliant work of investigative journalism.

Crawling into bed that night, she suddenly thought about something Detective Barker had told her months before. "This has thrown you for a loop," he'd said. "I think you want to make sense of it for yourself, not for any readers of the *Gazette*." She didn't know why that conversation popped into her head just then, but it made her uneasy. Her sister had said something very similar. They'd both been right, of course. Nicole had maintained her professionalism throughout the entire investigation, or at least she thought she had. Still, she had to admit that the series of deaths had unnerved her. They *didn't* make sense. How *can* life be so random? she wondered.

Now she had an answer of sorts. The events of that summer were not random. They made sense, after all; the events were explained by a force of evil. But that's exactly what was making her uneasy. Somehow, she had taken comfort in that. Randomness, she began to realize, was more disturbing to her than evil. There was no power over the arbitrary, but perhaps evil could be controlled. But it was a thought that made her feel...unclean somehow.

She wondered, too, about her moral responsibility to help destroy the items that were in Elaine Wilson's storage unit. She'd warned Elaine, but Elaine hadn't wanted to hear it. And now what could she do? Break into the storage unit and steal the boxes? Obviously, she'd be the prime suspect. Getting arrested for burglary sure didn't seem like a very good career move. No, the items were going to have to stay where they were. And as long as they were locked up in a storage unit, what difference did it make? In time, the evil would probably wear off.

Nicole closed her eyes and eventually drifted off to sleep. Several hours later, she was awakened by a howling windstorm. She could hear the gusts outside shaking the trees. In time, she managed to fall back to sleep and when she awoke in the morning, the sun was shining through the windows.

Nicole rose and strolled into the kitchen to make some coffee. She glanced at the calendar on the kitchen wall and remembered that this was no ordinary day. This was her birthday. With all that had been going on, she'd almost forgotten. The article, and everything that it represented, had been absorbing her time and energy. She sometimes felt as if she'd put her entire soul into the piece. She had plans for dinner and drinks that evening with some friends and she was looking forward to it. It had been a while since she'd cut loose and she was ready for some fun. She imagined she'd be hearing from her sister sometime, too. Kelly would never forget her little sister's birthday.

Nicole stirred her coffee and glanced out at the backyard and that's when she noticed that the previous night's windstorm had wreaked some damage. In fact, a large branch from an elm tree had apparently broken off and landed right on top of her patio table. She slid the fractured back door open and stepped outside, noticing that not only had the branch hit the table, it had shattered the glass top.

Nicole stood for a moment surveying the scene, thoughts of broken glass now coalescing in her mind—broken drinking glasses, broken sliding glass doors, broken table tops. This was getting weird. Before everything had happened, she probably wouldn't have given the matter any thought. It was coincidence. Now, she wondered if she even believed in coincidences anymore.

She shook the thoughts off and went back inside. She'd deal with the branch and the table later. Now, she needed to get ready for work. She was going to march into Walt's office and hand him the article, all printed out. Old school. Maybe Walt would appreciate it more that way.

She put her coffee cup down on the kitchen counter and went into her bedroom just as her phone rang.

"Happy birthday, Nickie!" came Kelly's cheery voice.

"Hey, Kel. Thanks! I knew you wouldn't forget."

"Of course not. And, hey, sorry again about not being able to make it tonight. If it was anything else, I'd cancel, but since I'm in the wedding, I guess I can't skip out on the rehearsal dinner."

"No problem, I understand."

"Maybe dinner next week somewhere?"

"Sure, that would be great."

"In the meantime, I've got a little surprise birthday present for you."

"Oh, yeah? You didn't have to get me anything."

"I couldn't resist. And guess what? It's in your house right now."

"What? In the house? Where?"

"Hall closet," Kelly chuckled. "I snuck in last week with the spare key. Hope you don't mind. I didn't want you to not have anything to open on your birthday. Go get it!"

Nicole smiled and strode out to the hall and opened the door to the closet, a closet of odds and ends that she rarely used. Sure enough, leaning against the wall was a large, wrapped package.

"What is it?!" she said into her phone.

"Open it!"

Nicole took the package out to the living room and sat down on the sofa. She carefully unwrapped the paper and soon she found herself looking at a stained-glass picture of a starfish.

"Kel, it's beautiful!"

"I thought you'd like it. It's an antique."

But at that moment, something about the picture gave Nicole a chill. She looked at it closer and realized with a jolt that she'd seen it before somewhere. In an instant, it occurred to her just where.

"Kelly," she said, speaking slowly, "can I ask where you bought this?"

Kelly laughed. "Hey, it's not polite to ask, you know."

In a serious tone that took Kelly aback, Nicole said, "Please tell me where you got it, Kelly."

"Well, sure, Nicole, I mean, if you must know, I found it on eBay."

Nicole breathed a sigh of relief. The sigh of relief was short-lived.

"It's funny," Kelly continued, "but it turns out that the seller is local. A college student name Cara. Isn't that something?"

Nicole froze. "Cara?"

"Yes, I'll send you a link to her stuff if you want."

Nicole felt her heart racing. "And this thing has been here all week?"

"Sure, why?"

Nicole tried to answer, but couldn't. She was thinking of the broken drinking glasses and the broken sliding glass door and the broken tabletop. She was thinking about how there are no coincidences.

"Nicole? Are you still there? What's the matter?"

Nicole sat the stained-glass picture down. From directly above her, she heard a slow creaking noise. She looked up just as the skylight—fixed in place since the 1940s—broke its seams and came plummeting from the ceiling.

"Nicole?"

But all Kelly could hear was a scream: "*Oh, God!*"

And then silence.

23

Eleven-year-old Ben and his nine-year-old brother Lucas were thrilled when the package arrived at their Delray Beach, Florida home. Just in time for Christmas! The boys had diligently saved their money—fifteen dollars—and had bought their mother the perfect Christmas gift, something she'd been talking about getting for some time, but Ben and Lucas were afraid it wasn't going to arrive in time.

"I told you it would get here," said Ted Duncan, the boys' father. "And your mom's going to love it. Now, let's get it wrapped and hide it away before she gets home from work!" It was Ted who actually found the gift and it was Ted's credit card that was used to make the purchase. But he took the money from the boys as reimbursement and was proud of them for having saved their money and for suggesting the idea in the first place. And it was a wonderful bargain.

Ted grabbed the wrapping paper and the three of them made short work of the project, with Lucas insisting on a big red bow to finish it off.

On Christmas morning, Amy was genuinely delighted when she opened up her gift from the boys. "Thank you both so much!" she exclaimed. "It's just what I wanted. I can't wait to try it out!"

The boys, of course, had their own share of gifts to open that morning. Of particular interest was the Big Kahuna inflatable pool slide for their swimming pool. Leading up to Christmas, they had bugged their parents incessantly for one.

After everything had been opened, the boys ran off to the back yard while the parents began to pick up all the wrapping paper.

"I think they liked everything," Ted smiled to his wife. "Did you see how wide their eyes got when they opened the box with the slide?"

"I know! And they were so good about getting us gifts. To think that they saved up and bought me something so useful. They're really good kids, Ted."

"We are truly lucky. And your gift was all their idea, you know. I mean, I helped them find it, but they were the ones who insisted on it."

"That's great. Well, where did you find it anyway?"

"Ha! Where else? Online. Someone was selling it on eBay and I jumped right on it."

"Well, I'm going to try it out right now," Amy declared. Then she took it into the kitchen. Ted loved seeing his wife so happy. He had gotten her an expensive watch, but she was just as thrilled with the gift from the boys. Who would have thought? Fifteen bucks. For an ice maker! One hell of a bargain.

Author's Thanks

If I truly wanted to thank my editor properly, that would need to be a short book all its own! It really is one thing to come up with a concept and a whole other thing to move it from mind to paper. I cannot thank you enough, Jerry Payne, for working alongside me this past year and helping me bring this book to life. You are brilliant and then some. Often times I look back at our countless email exchanges and am so very proud at what we've accomplished. I knew we could do it. Thanks, especially, for trusting my instincts on certain ideas that I know you initially thought might have been a bit out there. Your open-mindedness was invaluable for the creative process. Thank you, thank you, thank you for all your help. I can't wait for us to begin our next masterpiece!

www.ingramcontent.com/pod-product-compliance
Lightning Source LLC
Chambersburg PA
CBHW020154310726
48970CB00006B/2148